DATE			

LIGHTS OUT!

A bold money-making scheme spins wildly out of control in this absorbing thriller.

Desperate to escape his loveless marriage and embark on a new life in Argentina with the beautiful Gina Ellanado, Canadian engineer Carlton Smythe devises an audacious money-making scheme. But to pull it off, he'll need to do business with reputed local Mafia boss Dominick Martone. And that's when things spiral wildly out of control.

Recent Books by Donald Bain

The Margaret Truman Capital Crime
Series
EXPERIMENT IN MURDER

The *Murder, She Wrote* series
CLOSE-UP ON MURDER
PRESCRIPTION FOR MURDER
DOMESTIC MALICE
TROUBLE AT HIGH TIDE
THE FINE ART OF MURDER

LIGHTS OUT!

Donald Bain

Severn House Large Print
London & New York

This first large print edition published 2014
in Great Britain and the USA by
SEVERN HOUSE PUBLISHERS LTD of
19 Cedar Road, Sutton, Surrey, England, SM2 5DA.
First world regular print edition published 2014 by
Severn House Publishers Ltd., London and New York.

British Library Cataloguing in Publication Data

Bain, Donald, 1935- author.
  Lights out!
  1. Mafia--Fiction. 2. Suspense fiction. 3. Large type
  books.
  I. Title
  813.5'4-dc23

ISBN-13: 9780727897572

For my best friend, Renée, who also happens to be my talented wife.

For my agent, Bob Diforio of the D4EO Literary Agency, who has given me a new lease on my writing career.

And for all the Smythes out there ... and the women who've ended up with a Smythe in their lives.

'Nothing defines humans more than their willingness to do irrational things in the pursuit of phenomenally unlikely pay-offs. This is the principle behind lotteries, dating, and religion.'

Scott Adams

ONE

He'd just dropped his drawers when the lights went out.

The plunge into darkness was so abrupt that it was almost audible. One minute his hotel room overlooking Times Square had been bathed in soft, yellow light from floor lamps mixed with the glow from the TV screen on which an adult movie played. Now, everything was black.

He pulled up his boxers, decorated with little red-and-white Canadian maple leafs, and went to the window. A moment ago, the neon lights on the streets below had dazzled, but now the only illumination came from the chaotic movement of automobile headlights.

'Good evening, Mr Smith,' said the desk clerk who answered his call.

'It's Smythe. Like Blithe. *Blithe Spirit?*'

'Yes, sir, Mr Smythe. There's been a black-out.'

'City-wide?'

'I don't know, sir. It will probably be over soon.'

'I certainly hope so.'

Smythe felt his way across the room, found the small transistor radio he always traveled with, and tuned to a local all-news station that had gone to auxiliary generators. He plopped on the bed and listened to the announcer: 'The blackout appears to have affected all areas of the city. I've just been handed a report that this power outage extends into Queens and Staten Island. Police and fire units have been—' A burst of static drowned him out.

Smythe flipped on his cell phone. The battery was low and there was no way to recharge it. Even if he could, cellular transmitters would have only a few hours of battery backup before they, too, gave out. He called home.

'Where are you?' his wife asked.

'New York.'

'I thought you were coming back today.'

'My meetings ran longer than expected and—'

'You know we're having guests tomorrow night.'

'Yes, Cynthia, I know that. I'll try and catch the earliest plane in the morning. It depends on how long this blackout lasts. I'm sure all flights are cancelled – the airports are dark – they'll be backed up. I'm not sure that—'

'What dreadful timing,' she said.

10

'I'll do my best.'

'Think of something, Carlton. The mayor and his wife are coming and—'

Smythe held the phone away and made a harsh squawking sound.

'Carlton?'

Another squawk from him. 'Battery running l-o-w – losing p-o-w-e-r. *Squawk, squawk.*'

He closed the phone. He knew the landline phone in the room would work but didn't pick it up. Instead, he returned to the window and watched the erratic jumble of traffic below, headlamps bunching up at intersections, the faint wail of sirens penetrating the hotel window's allegedly soundproof glass.

He pulled a small penlight from his travel kit and used it to illuminate the dial on the room's wired phone. It took a while to get through the voicemail's myriad prompts until a live person at Air Canada spoke.

'Is it possible to book an early morning flight to Toronto?' Smythe asked.

'Everything is down, sir, the computers – there's a blackout.'

'I know that,' Smythe said, trying to keep pique out of his voice, 'but can't you reserve a flight for when it ends?'

'You'll have to call again when that happens, sir. I'm unable to—'

Smythe quietly placed the handset into its

cradle. At least he could tell Cynthia that he'd tried to get home for the party. He wasn't unhappy about missing it – another party, another dull round of conversation with Toronto's movers-and-shakers, their place on Cynthia's invitation list determined by the position they occupied in the city's social and leadership hierarchy.

He stretched out on the bed. Ironic, he thought, to be the victim of a blackout. He'd spent his entire professional career working as an engineer for Power-Can, a huge Ontario power company on the outskirts of Toronto. Until his dismissal eighteen months earlier he'd been instrumental in calling for fail-safe procedures at the plant in the hope of avoiding another blackout like the one in 2003 that had paralyzed much of the Mid-West and East Coast. He'd urged his employer to begin substituting a new generation of giant electronic switches for the increasingly inefficient mechanical ones that failed to react fast enough in the event of a power glitch that could, and had, within seconds, wreaked havoc with a large portion of the North American power grid. He'd been tenacious in calling for this change, evidently too much so for his bosses who called him in a year and a half ago to announce that he was being phased out. Downsized. Fired! The patronizing words of his boss had stayed with him to this day: 'Change is inevitable, Carlton. Spearheading teams these days takes the energy and drive of younger people, young Turks on their way up. It's time for you to enjoy the good life with that lovely wife of yours, travel, bask in your golden years.'

Golden Years? He'd just turned fifty-three.

'*You bastard!*' Smythe had wanted to say to his boss, a toad-like creature with a perpetual crooked smile. But he didn't. He accepted the buyout and packed up his office, his smiles to well-wishers masking his inner fury.

It had been a wrenching experience. He'd devoted the best years of his professional life to Power-Can, a dedicated and loyal employee who'd received numerous citations and promotions. Being summarily axed enraged this otherwise contented engineer. The severance package, generous by any standard, did nothing to mitigate his anger – and hurt.

He stewed about it for weeks in the home he and Cynthia shared in the prestigious Rosedale section of downtown Toronto. His dismay at being fired had nothing to do with money. He'd married into wealth. Cynthia Smythe's father had been Toronto's most successful venture capitalist. His firm, Wiggins Capital, had arranged funding for many of the city's largest renewal projects:

13

hotels, condominiums, office buildings. He was a power broker in Ontario politics, a king-maker of the first order, and never reluctant to let people know it.

Smythe closed his eyes and allowed his mind to wander. He wanted pleasant thoughts, but unpleasant ones kept bumping the good ones to the sidelines. As hard as he tried to avoid it, memories of one particular day many years ago took center-stage.

'I'll be straight with you, Smythe,' Walter Wiggins said as they sat at a table in a secluded corner of the National Club's Blake Lounge, 'I'm more than displeased that you've knocked up my little girl. In fact I'm pretty damned angry about it.'

The year was 1981. Carlton H. Smythe was within a month of graduating from Toronto University with a degree in electrical engineering from the School of Applied Science and Engineering. Cynthia Wiggins was also scheduled to graduate. Her degree was in opera performance from the university's esteemed Music Department. That she'd passed the audition and had been accepted into the program surprised everyone. Her voice was considered mediocre. Had her father's name on the university building he'd funded played a role in the decision? She preferred to think that it

14

hadn't; her father knew damn well that it had. In the end, it didn't matter. It was what his only daughter wanted, and that was good enough for Walter Wiggins.

Cynthia had met Carlton following a performance in the university's MacMillan Theatre. She'd had a small role in that evening's production of Mozart's *The Magic Flute*. She wasn't happy with the size of her part and pouted late into the evening at a pub frequented by art and music students. Carlton and his roommate had gone to the movies and stopped in at the bar on their way back to the dorm.

Carlton had met Cynthia before and considered her sexy in a non-glamorous way. She wouldn't win any beauty contests, but she had a nice smile, and all the female lumps were where they were supposed to be. He'd heard rumors that she was easy: 'Cynthia Roundheels' was the way a male student once characterized her to Smythe, perhaps unfairly, maybe not.

She was tipsy when Carlton started up a conversation at the bar. After a half hour she suggested that they go back to the apartment her father maintained for her to avoid, as she'd told him, 'those shallow, petty girls in the dorm.' Their clothes were off within minutes of walking through the door, and Smythe, who wasn't a virgin but whose sexual experiences were not of the notches-on-the-bedpost variety, found himself on top of the naked, aspiring diva, whose skin felt cold and clammy, and whose only words were, 'Do it deep and hard. Make me forget!'

He energetically tried to please, hoping for an audible sign from her that he'd succeeded. He heard a muted 'Oooh' just before he climaxed with a loud 'Aaah!' He rolled off and asked if it was good for her.

'Sure,' she said, sitting on a throw pillow to avoid staining the chair's fabric. Carlton took a matching chair across from her. She reached out with a leg and used her stubby, red-tipped toes to play with his flaccid penis.

'That was wonderful,' he said, almost thanking her but stopping himself. Maybe that wasn't the right thing to say.

She disappeared into the bathroom. He slipped on his briefs and shirt. Smythe was tall, skinny and pale, and uncomfortable sitting around naked. She returned with a marijuana cigarette she'd rolled in the bathroom, lit it, and handed it to him. He drew deeply, bringing on a coughing spasm. 'I don't do that much,' he explained, handing it back.

She laughed and finished the joint as they talked, she about her future career in opera, he about his ambitions to become an electrical engineer with a large company.

An hour later, he said, 'I'd better be going. I have an exam in the morning.'

She walked him to the door. 'Sure you don't want to do it again?' she asked.

'No, I don't think so. I mean, I'd love to but— I didn't use anything.'

'Huh?'

'I didn't use any protection. I hope—'

'Don't worry about it,' she said. 'It's my safe time.'

The waiter asked Walter Wiggins and Smythe for their orders.

'We'll both have warm chicken salad, and iced tea,' Wiggins said. The waiter walked away. 'Let me continue to be blunt,' Wiggins said to Smythe at their table in the exclusive club. 'Frankly – and I always believe in being frank – you're not the sort of husband I envisioned for Cynthia.'

'I'm really sorry that this has happened, sir,' Smythe said. 'It was an accident. Cynthia thought that she was in the safe period of her month and—'

'Cynthia wouldn't know her safe period from Christmas Day. She's talented – I'm sure you know that – but she lacks common sense. She gets that from her mother's side. Now, you strike me as a decent sort of chap. At least you've come forward like a man and taken responsibility.' He paused to chew his cheek. 'Smythe? English?'

17

'What? Oh, English and German. My father is—'

'Better than Lubinski or Luciano.'

'I never intended for Cynthia to get pregnant, Mr Wiggins.'

'Who the hell ever does? Look, I pride myself on being a realist. OK, you've knocked up my daughter and the two of you will get married. At least the kid will be legitimate.'

Smythe winced. 'Knocked up' seemed unnecessarily harsh.

'But I'll be damned if I'll stand by while my only daughter ends up in some tract house with a bunch of bawling babies crawling around.'

They were interrupted by the arrival of lunch. Smythe didn't like his chicken salad warm but knew better than to have ordered something else. All he wanted was to get through the meal, race outside, and breathe fresh air again. His future father-in-law was a suffocating presence, an octopus engulfing Smythe in its mass, cutting off breathing, making him sweat, and causing a rash to break out on his chest and back that he didn't dare scratch.

'Go ahead, eat,' Wiggins commanded. 'As I was saying, I want only the best for my little girl.'

Smythe thought of her playing with him with her toes: 'Deep and hard. Make me forget!'

If only forgetting were that easy.

'You strike me, Smythe, as someone who likes to do things,' Wiggins said between forkfuls of salad.

Smythe looked at him quizzically.

'That's not good,' Wiggins proclaimed, bringing his hand down on the table for emphasis.

'It's not?'

'No, it's not. The world is full of people like you who spend their lives *doing* things.'

'What, ah – what sort of things, Mr Wiggins?'

'It doesn't matter what they do. The point is that you'll never get anywhere *doing* things.' He lowered his voice and came forward. 'The way to get ahead is to be in a position to tell those people who do things *what* to do.' His expression demanded agreement.

'I think I see what you mean,' Smythe said.

'I'll give you an example. You plan to be an engineer. OK, we need engineers. But what I want for my future son-in-law is to be in a position to tell other engineers what to do. The big picture, Carlton. Bottom-line.'

'That makes sense to me,' said Carlton, sipping his iced tea.

'And I won't settle for anything less for my little girl.'

Smythe nodded.

19

'We'll start with your clothes.'

Smythe looked down at his shirtfront. He'd worn his best suit to this command lunch, a light gray one that had recently been cleaned and pressed. His shirt was white – both of his dress shirts were white – and he'd chosen an aqua tie that he thought went nicely with the suit.

'That thing you have in your shirt pocket,' Wiggins said.

Smythe again glanced down.

'That plastic thing with those pens and ... what is that, a slide rule? I'll be honest with you, Smythe. No offense, but it looks stupid.'

'I'm not offended, Mr Wiggins.'

Let me out of here.

'I'll take you to Trend Custom Tailors. Tommy Battista's a friend. We'll get you outfitted like the leader I know you'll become.'

'That's very generous of you, sir.'

'As I said, I want only the best for my little girl. Finished? I have a board meeting to get to.'

Wiggins's limo stood running outside the club. He offered to drop Smythe anywhere he wished, but Carlton made an excuse to decline the ride.

'I'm glad we had this man-to-man talk, Smythe. Mrs Wiggins has already got things moving for the wedding and reception. Any

20

questions?'

'No, sir, no questions.'

'Good.' He gripped Smythe's right hand in his and brought his other hand down hard on his bony shoulder. 'Welcome to the family, son.'

Smythe was asleep in his Manhattan hotel room when the lights came back on. He awoke, sat up and stared at the TV screen where two naked women were coiled around each other. He glanced at the clock radio. The blackout had lasted less than an hour. He called Air Canada again and booked a flight to Toronto, leaving LaGuardia at eleven the following morning. After watching the movie for a few minutes, he turned off the set and lights, and pulled the covers up around him. Memories of his entrance into the Wiggins family, and his thirty-year marriage to the failed opera singer, had been too exhausting to think of anything but sleep.

TWO

Smythe had made it home in time for the party following the blackout.

Now, almost a year later, he'd barely gotten back to Toronto for yet another of Cynthia's soirees. This time, a blackout hadn't been the stumbling block.

'Cynthia was so concerned that you wouldn't be back in time for the party,' Cynthia's mother said as guests left the dinner table and repaired to a drawing room for coffee, dessert, and after-dinner drinks. Mrs Wiggins was now a widow, her husband Walter having choked to death on a piece of warm chicken salad at the National Club.

'I wasn't sure I'd make it,' Carlton said. 'My flight from Buenos Aires was delayed because of the weather.'

'How's the consulting business, Carlton?' a male guest asked.

'Couldn't be better, Harold. My client in Argentina keeps me hopping, eats up most of my time.'

The truth was that the Argentinean Power Authority had informed him three weeks after his presentation to them that they'd decided to hire someone else.

'Carlton, darling,' Cynthia said, 'Mrs Kalich didn't put out sugar for the coffee. Please go tell her we need it, and need it now.'

He excused himself and went to the kitchen where he delivered the message to their housekeeper. He rejoined the guests and was asked again how his consulting business was progressing.

'Good,' he said. 'Just fine.'

The man lowered his voice. 'How are those hot-blooded Argentinean *señoritas*, Carlton?' He punctuated it with a jab to the ribs.

'Afraid I'm too busy when I'm there for anything like that,' Smythe offered, not entirely convincing.

'If you say so, buddy,' the man said, walking away after delivering a final, knowing leer.

Smythe's travels were brought up again a few minutes later, this time in Cynthia's mother's presence.

'So much traveling,' Mrs Wiggins said. 'Poor Cynthia. She's so often alone and with this big house to run.'

'Where are you off to next?' Carlton was asked.

'Back to Argentina in a few days.'

'I don't see why you had to go all the way

to Argentina to find a client,' Mrs Wiggins said. 'How many trips there has it been? Seven? Eight? Cynthia is dying to go with you. When are you planning to—?'

'Seven, Mother,' Smythe said through a forced smile. He'd become practiced at forced smiles.

'There should be plenty of business for you right here in Toronto,' Mrs Wiggins threw in.

Smythe changed the subject to the Toronto Blue Jays' chances that baseball season. Cynthia questioned why anyone would bother watching a baseball game. 'I've never understood the appeal,' she said, which prompted the mayor to extol the virtues of sporting events, especially how the revenue they generated benefited everyone in the city.

'Cynthia is one of the primary supporters of COC,' Mrs Wiggins proudly told the mayor.

'The largest opera company in Canada,' Cynthia amplified.

'I never miss a performance,' the mayor's wife said.

'I've attended a few,' said the mayor.

'Yes, *only* a few,' his wife chided.

And so went the conversation for the rest of that evening – baseball, opera, travels, the United States' perceived arrogance in prohibiting Americans from buying prescription drugs from Canada: 'They import all sorts of tainted products from China and other third-world countries,' the mayor said, 'but treat us like a banana republic.'

Everyone agreed.

The guests eventually departed, leaving Carlton, Cynthia and her mother in the house with Mrs Kalich, who set about cleaning up the drawing room. The mother planned to stay the night, as she often did following Cynthia's dinner parties.

'I'll be out in my office,' Carlton announced.

'At this hour, Carlton?' Mrs Wiggins said

'He smokes his vile cigars out there,' Cynthia said.

'A disgusting habit,' her mother agreed. 'Walter smoked them. I'm certain they hastened his death.'

Carlton smiled graciously. 'I just have a few loose ends to tie up,' he said. 'Another wonderful party, Cynthia.' He kissed her cheek and headed for the kitchen where a door led to their handsomely planted and lighted rear yard. A free-form swimming pool occupied the rear-most portion of the property. Next to it was a two-room pool house. One room was a cabana, fitted out with benches, pegs upon which to hang clothing, and a series of shelves holding beach towels. Smythe had converted the second room into an office. There was a

25

phone, a combination fax/scanner/printer, a laptop computer, a few putty-colored file cabinets, a wall calendar, a cordless telephone, and a small desk whose surface was illuminated by two gooseneck halogen lamps. Heavy gold curtains covered a single window that looked out over the gardens.

He crossed the grounds, entered the pool house, closed and locked the door, and sat. He loosened his tie, came forward with his elbows on the desk, and held his head in his hands. He'd found the evening to be excruciatingly precious and uninteresting, and hoped that Cynthia and the guests hadn't seen him constantly consulting his watch.

He turned on the computer. As he waited for it to boot up, he reached into the lower drawer of one of the file cabinets, slid file folders forward, and grabbed another folder that lay flat beneath the vertical ones. He placed it on the desk, went to the window where he parted the curtains to ensure that no one was heading his way, closed them, and opened the folder. Staring up at him was an eight-by-ten color photograph of a strikingly beautiful woman. Her hair was inky-black, her eyes equally dark – and impressively large. Her blood-red lips were full, her teeth glistening white against flawless burnished skin.

He let out an involuntary groan of pleasure. 'Gina!'

Accompanying the photograph were handwritten notes in Spanish on scented pastel paper. He understood most of the words, especially ones of endearment: *Adorable, Irresistible, Mi bella amada, Querida, Me desespero cuando estás lejos.*

After a glance at the door, he logged on to AOL and in the address line wrote, *Gina Ellanado.* The message box appeared. He pulled from a desk drawer an English-Spanish dictionary and *The Lover's Dictionary* which translated lovers' words into four languages. He'd come across it while browsing a used book store in New York shortly after meeting her.

Using those resources, he began to compose his message to the woman in the picture: *Eres la chica más guapa del mundo.* It wasn't an overstatement. Gina Ellanado *was* the most beautiful woman in the world, in *his* world. He repeated the phrase from one of her notes to him: *Me desespero cuando estás lejos.* It was true. He was desperate when she was away from him. Tired of translating, he turned to English: *Soon, my darling, we shall be in each others' arms again.* He spelled out his upcoming travel plans to Argentina, and ended with, *I count the seconds until we are together.*

He sent the message, deleted it from the 'Sent' file, checked to be sure that he'd erased her most recent message from that

27

morning, and signed off. He next brought up a folder labeled 'Franchise' and opened it. A series of screen pages emerged from the file. Some were filled with notes of a technical nature, the others columns of dollar figures linked to geographical locations. He typed in a few additional thoughts, closed the file, shut down the computer, chose an expensive Cuban cigar from a small leather humidor, carefully lit it so that the flame of the match never actually touched its end, sat back, propped his feet on the desk, and smiled legitimately for the first time that evening.

THREE

Carlton Smythe's metamorphosis had blossomed during his first trip to Buenos Aires nine months ago.

He settled into the wide, soft leather seat in First Class of the Aerolíneas Argentinas 747 that prepared to leave the gate at New York's JFK airport. He'd opted to fly to New York from Toronto to catch the Argentinean airline rather than depart from Calgary. The Argentinean national airline's use of the wide-body 747 and its reputation for pampering in First Class appealed.

This initial trip to Argentina had been for legitimate business reasons. He'd learned that the Argentinean government was looking for engineering help to implement a proposed plan to improve its power-generating capacity. He'd contacted the appropriate people and was invited to make a presentation.

He checked into an Executive Suite at the Four Seasons in Buenos Aires, next to the exclusive La Recoleta district. After becoming acclimatized to the suite – it was spacious and handsomely furnished and decorated, with a fine view of the fountain and the city beyond – he unpacked and decided to have a drink in Le Dôme, a bar off the lobby, and an early dinner in the hotel's Le Mistral restaurant. He was tired from the long flight and wanted some rehearsal time in the suite before his presentation the following morning.

Le Dôme was bustling. Smythe found an unoccupied table near the end of the bar, ordered a gin-and-tonic and sat back, happy to have arrived and excited about the possibility of landing his first client. He'd purchased a Cuban cigar from the front desk, now he lit it, and amused himself by watching the comings-and-goings of bar patrons, a mix of visiting businessmen and locals. Everyone was well-dressed; Smythe was pleased that he'd stayed in his suit and tie.

He was about to finish his drink and move to Le Mistral when she walked into the bar. He wasn't the only man to take notice of Gina Ellanado. She stood at the entrance and looked around as though searching for someone. She carried a shopping bag; an alligator purse dangled from one shoulder. Her aqua dress was low-cut, its hem slightly above the knee. Smythe hoped she wouldn't notice how intently he stared at her and shifted his eyes, but only for a second. She navigated tables and headed in his direction, stopping a few feet away.

'*Si?*' the bartender said.

She shook her head and turned. As she did, her shopping bag swung around and knocked over a small vase of flowers on Smythe's table. He was quick enough to keep it from going over the edge, and righted it.

'*Perdón,*' she said.

'*De nada,*' he replied, using one of the Spanish phrases he'd learned in preparation for his trip.

'I am – how do you say it? – I am clumsy,' she said.

'No, you're not,' he said, standing. 'Would you like to sit?'

Did the expression on her face indicate that he was being too forward? Evidently not because she smiled – he'd never seen such a smile – and sat in the chair he pulled out, the shopping bag and purse on the floor beside her.

'Well,' he said. 'Well, ah, my name is Carlton. Carlton Smythe. Ah, *¿cómo estás?*'

A tinkling laugh accompanied her smile. '*Muy bien, gracias.* You are an American?'

'That's right. *Si.* Are you from here, from Buenos Aires?'

She nodded and looked away. He took that moment to fix on her cleavage. There was plenty to admire.

When she returned her attention to him, he asked if she would like a drink.

'Yes, thank you.'

'You speak English.'

She fluttered her nicely manicured hands, her nails tipped in crimson to match her lipstick. 'So-so,' she said, 'a little, sometimes not so good.'

'You speak very good English,' he said, motioning for the waiter who took her order of *cerveza*.

Her choice of a drink pleased Smythe. He too enjoyed an occasional glass of beer but there was never any in the house, Cynthia having ruled it *déclassé*. It was nice to see a woman order it, and for a moment he considered offering her a cigar.

They clicked the rims of their glasses, and Smythe ordered a second drink. She sipped her beer; the sight of her tongue darting out occasionally to wipe foam from her lips was highly erotic, her perfume intoxicating.

Conversation became easier; she spoke better English than she gave herself credit for. Some things said in combination English and Spanish went past Smythe, but he was certain they weren't terribly important. He learned that she lived in Buenos Aires, and was a consultant to a cosmetics company. He told her of his own consulting firm and that he was in Argentina to meet with government officials involved with the country's power industry. She listened intently to what he had to say, her large – huge – almost black eyes opened wide as though his words were the most important words she'd ever heard. At one point, she moved so that her leg touched his. He withdrew his leg for an instant but allowed it to settle back against her.

'Would you like another beer?' he asked.

'Yes, but I must be leaving soon.'

'Oh? I thought we might have dinner together, here at the hotel?'

It occurred to him earlier that she could be a prostitute. If so, he decided that he would pay the price.

'Dinner?' she said, frowning. She glanced at her watch. 'Yes, all right. I would like that very much.'

They were seated in a corner of Le Mistral, its walls and chairs covered in leather, candlelit tables augmenting soft light from Tiffany chandeliers. A harpist added to the decidedly romantic atmosphere.

'Would you like wine,' he asked, 'or another beer?'

'What do you say?' she asked.

'Me? Oh, I'll have wine or—no, you decide. I leave it up to you. This is your place, your country.'

She ordered a bottle of Malbec, explaining to Smythe that it was a popular Argentinean wine that went well with beef.

'Argentinean beef,' he said. 'The best.'

'Very good,' she agreed. 'So, Mr Carlton, tell me about you.'

'Carlton is my first name,' he said. 'There isn't much to tell. As I said, I'm an engineer and have my own business. Consulting. Like you.'

They conversed easily during dinner – a New York strip steak with a thick herb sauce, *chimichurri*, for him, a Mediterranean fish stew for her. The bottle of wine was soon emptied, and a second ordered, which they also finished. His two drinks in the bar, and the wine, had their predictable effect on him, although he was not as inebriated as he might have been under other circumstances. He felt good, relaxed and carefree. Gina had contributed to his feeling of wellbeing by proving to be a superb listener as he wove stories about himself, some true, others embellished if not outright lies.

'Are you married, Mr Carlton Smythe?' she asked matter-of-factly at one point, taking his left hand in hers and running her index finger around his ring finger.

'Yes,' he replied. 'But my marriage is— well, it will be ending soon.'

'I am sorry,' she said.

'Yes, it's sad,' he said, trying to formulate what to say that would not sound too self-serving, yet make a pending divorce under-standable. 'My business takes me away from home a lot,' he offered, 'and my wife resents it. She doesn't understand my business, or me. She's a—she's a good woman, but we've agreed that it will be better to go our separate ways.'

'You have children?'

'No.'

'That is good. It is the children who suffer.'

'Are you married?' he asked.

'No. I have not found the right man.'

With that topic out of the way, her warmth toward him increased with each glass of wine, and they might have been mistaken for newly-weds.

Decision time. Should he invite her up to his room?

'I must go,' she said suddenly, as though reading his mind and heading off that possibility.

'Of course.' He stood and pulled out her chair. 'May I accompany you home?'

'Oh, no, no, no,' she said. 'But I thank you for suggesting. *Gracias.*'

'*De nada.*'

They left Le Mistral and walked to the street.

It had started to rain lightly.

'It is good,' she said, 'for the flowers.'

'Yes, for the flowers.'

She pulled a small umbrella from her bag and popped it open.

'Are you sure I can't see you home?'

Her response was to raise her face and kiss him. He allowed his tongue to slip between her teeth, and she pressed her pelvis against him. Would she be offended by his erection? he wondered.

'I must see you again,' he said once they'd disengaged.

'I would like that very much.'

He told her his room number and asked her to call him the next day. She did, and they met for dinner. Following a tango show at an upscale bar, she persuaded him to join her on the dance floor. He knew he looked awkward, even silly, but he was powerless to resist. They shopped together; he bought her an emerald ring. One night, during heavier rain, they paraded together down the *Avenida 9 de Julio*, the widest boulevard on the planet, and he was tempted to emulate Gene Kelly in *Singin' in the Rain*, to take her umbrella and dance. But he was afraid that he would fall into a puddle and make a fool of himself.

He worried about how he might look, too, when they climbed naked into the king-sized bed in his hotel room on their third night together. He'd tried to induce her into bed on the second night but she'd resisted, which only added to her appeal. That she was no easy mark boosted her character quotient in Smythe's eyes. This was a woman to be viewed not only as a sexual object, she was worthy of love – and Carlton Smythe, married Canadian out-of-work electrical engineer, had fallen head-over-heels in love.

She praised his lovemaking that night which spurred him on, the wild abandon with which she offered herself, the sweet smell of her, the groans of pleasure mingled with satisfied laughter, sweaty and slippery and altogether a woman, *his* woman.

He'd told her following their lovemaking that he had to return to Canada to pursue a major business deal worth millions. 'But I shall return!' he said with dramatic flourish, thinking of Douglas MacArthur's famous pledge to return to the Philippines. 'I shall return to see *you* again, Gina Ellanado.'

'And I shall be here waiting for you.'

She declined to stay the night with him, and he escorted her to a waiting taxi.

'I leave in the morning,' he said.

She nodded.

'But I will be back.'

'You must,' she said.

'I will. You have my word.'

'Tell me about your presentation,' Cynthia said to Carlton the morning following his return from that first trip to Argentina. They sat in the kitchen.

'It was successful, Cynthia, very successful. They really liked my experience and my ideas. I'm sure they'll buy my proposition.' It really didn't matter to him whether they did or not. He would return to Buenos Aires regardless of the outcome.

'That's good,' she said.

'Of course, it will mean having to go to Buenos Aires quite a bit.'

She nodded, and topped off her cup of coffee from a carafe on the table.

'I know you aren't happy when I travel but—'

'I have an idea,' she said.

'Oh?'

'I can come with you to Argentina. I've always wanted to see South America. It would be a vacation trip. Oh, you can conduct your business, but we can stay a few extra days and enjoy ourselves.'

'I think that's ... I think that's a great idea,' he said. 'Maybe after I've gotten acclimated with my new clients and won't have to spend day and night with them.'

He finished what was left in his cup. 'I think I'll hit the gym,' he said.

'That's good,' she said. 'Oh, there's a press reception at COC tomorrow night. We're promoting the next opera. We're doing *Carmen*. You'll come with me? I know you're tired from your trip but—'

'Of course I'll come with you,' he said. *Keep her happy.*

FOUR

Celeste Aida drifted up from downstairs to the bathroom where Smythe stood naked in front of the mirror. It was Cynthia's favorite aria; she started many mornings singing it while moving through the large house. Smythe was indifferent to opera and opera singers, and found excuses to not accompany his wife to performances.

But her position on the board of the Canadian Opera Company involved many evenings entertaining cast members at home, which invariably ended up with impromptu recitals that included Cynthia. Smythe had no basis upon which to judge her voice. It seemed to him that she sounded pretty much like all the other sopranos, no better or worse than those gathered around the grand piano at these domestic musicales. On the evenings he was present, he joined the enthusiastic, non-performing handclappers urging the singers and musicians to greater heights.

He examined himself in the mirror. He'd recently lost weight around his middle, an inch in his estimation, and his arms seemed to have developed slightly more definition thanks to light weightlifting in their home gym. Cynthia had been surprised at his sudden interest in physical fitness, and said so. He responded, 'I'm getting older, Cynthia. I think it's time I paid a little more attention to my health.' She said she thought that was a wise decision and the subject was not brought up again.

He'd been using a shampoo and conditioner that promised to add body to his silken gray hair, much of which had disappeared from the top of his head. Was it working? He preferred to believe that it was. He'd allowed it to grow longer at the sides and in the back, to Cynthia's chagrin: 'You look like some aging hippie,' she'd commented.

'Just an experiment,' he'd said. 'I'll get a haircut soon.'

Which he did, but instructed the barber to keep the sides and back long. 'Just going back to my hippie days,' he said, joining the barber in a good laugh.

After showering, he came downstairs wearing a pale blue silk robe over pale blue silk pajamas. Cynthia was in the kitchen with her mother.

'Good morning,' Smythe said cheerily.

'Good morning, Carlton,' the mother said, not looking up from that morning's copy of the *Globe and Mail.*

He came up behind Cynthia at the sink, kissed the back of her head, and joined his mother-in-law at the table.

Cynthia turned, arms folded. 'Carlton, I need to talk to you.'

'Sure,' he said, pouring coffee into his cup.

'I really don't see any reason for you to be making all these trips to South America.'

'I told you, Cynthia, that I've developed this very close and lucrative relationship with my clients in Buenos Aires. They need nurturing, a lot of hand-holding, and I don't want to lose this account.'

'There are plenty of clients right here in Canada,' she said, echoing her mother.

'And I'm pursuing them, too.'

'Frankly,' said Cynthia, 'I don't see why you're bothering becoming a consultant, or whatever it is you call it. Just handling the family finances should be job enough. Besides, I need you here. We are coming into a very busy social season and—'

'I appreciate what you're saying, Cynthia, but I'm not ready to retire and sit around doing the family books and playing host to half of Toronto.'

Mrs Wiggins looked up over half-glasses as Cynthia let out a frustrated grunt and stomped from the kitchen.

'I wish she understood my needs,' Smythe said to his mother-in-law.

41

'What about *her* needs, Carlton?'

'I'm well aware of Cynthia's needs, Mom, and I always try to meet them.'

Mrs Wiggins sighed deeply and closed the paper. She removed her glasses and used them as a prop as she turned to face him. The sermon was about to begin. 'I know I shouldn't become involved in your marital situation, Carlton, but I feel I must. Surely you're sensitive to what Cynthia has had to live through since the miscarriage?'

Cynthia had miscarried the child conceived during that chance sexual encounter in her student apartment. It happened the week after she and Carlton were married in a lavish ceremony and reception at her parents' home. An added medical complication necessitated the removal of her reproductive organs. There would never be children unless they opted to adopt, which was anathema to Cynthia: 'Who knows what we might end up with, someone else's problem, like buying a used car.'

The notion of adopting a child was dropped.

'That was more than thirty years ago, Mom.' Smythe was never sure whether to address her as Mom, Mum, Ma'am or Mother. Using her first name, Gladys, was out of the question.

'Something that traumatic lasts a lifetime,' she said. 'Cynthia has had to live with memories of that for the rest of her life.'

'I was impacted by it, too,' Smythe said, not pleased that he found himself defending himself to this old lady who raised self-righteousness to a new level.

'Of course you were, dear.'

Don't call me dear.

'The point, Carlton, is that Cynthia needs you here more than you need to be winging all over the world looking for clients. You must admit that had you listened to Walter and come to work for him, you wouldn't be in this unfortunate position.'

'I—'. He stood. 'I'm sure you're right, Mom, but it's important that I pursue something meaningful to me.'

'I should think that managing the significant money left to Cynthia by her father – money that you enjoy, too, Carlton – would provide enough of a professional challenge.'

'I really don't think that—'

'And,' she said, not missing a beat, 'it would help you to satisfy your middle-aged insecurities.'

He looked down at her.

'I understand that men go through what's called a mid-life crisis. Fortunately, Walter was too grounded to allow that to happen. But—'

'Excuse me,' Smythe said, 'I have work to do.'

He'd vowed years ago not to get into an

argument with Gladys Wiggins, and had been successful for the most part. But there were times. A fleeting vision of being behind bars for murder, and being sexually assaulted by brutish, tattooed inmates, came and went.

As he dressed in his bedroom – he and Cynthia had separate bedrooms – a familiar and unwelcome feeling overcame him. He had various names for it, but they were only euphemistic rationalizations. The truth was, guilt often descended upon him like a gigantic yoke that threatened to press him into the ground.

He sat on the edge of his bed and waited for the feeling to pass, or at least to wane. That burden of guilt was heavy, and he sometimes wondered whether the course he'd set out on at this stage of his life was worth it.

He'd initiated an affair, the first in his married life. He had myriad reasons to excuse himself his indiscretions, and freely invoked them. He was involved in a loveless marriage, with a woman to whom he had pledged his lifetime allegiance. It was easy for him to assign blame to her for their marriage having become one of convenience, but he knew that was wrong and self-serving. Cynthia was simply the product of her overbearing mother and father, and Smythe and his wife saw the world through different eyes. Did he hate her? His answer to that question was always an emphatic no. Cynthia didn't deserve hatred, nor did her family. Hatred was, he believed, a religious concept, and Smythe was not a religious man. Cynthia was an Episcopalian by birth, although Carlton knew that neither her mother and father, nor their daughter, attended services in search of divine inspiration and deliverance. They went to church because it was part of their social fabric; it was expected of them, and the Episcopal Church was an appropriate choice in Anglo-Toronto where the religion you embraced helped define your social class.

Now and then, Carlton accompanied Cynthia to church on Sunday mornings. Until meeting Gina Ellanado, his main concern had been staying awake. Now, he wondered whether the priest could see into his soul, read something in his eyes or posture that shouted *adulterer!* He wasn't literally afraid that this might be the case. Carlton didn't believe in God and was a firm advocate of evolution: 'We're just a two-legged species of the animal kingdom,' was what he liked to think, and sometimes said to friends. He wasn't concerned that he might go to Hell because of having broken his marriage vows. There was no Heaven and Hell, was how he saw it.

Still, there was the guilt, call it shame, that

consumed him at odd times of the day or night, and in a variety of places – like church, or the supermarket, or in the midst of a party while sopranos and tenors filled the house with their voices. But never when wrapped in Gina's soft, scented flesh. Never then.

He chose a dark blue suit from a closet full of custom suits from Trend Custom Tailors, a freshly ironed pale blue shirt, and muted red tie. He didn't need to dress up for the day but felt more comfortable – more justified – in the eyes of his wife and her mother if he did. He returned to the kitchen and had it to himself. He ate a bowl of cereal, washed down a handful of vitamins and an Aleve for arthritic pains that had recently developed, and went to a first floor room which functioned as another office from which he oversaw the management of the family's considerable finances. A pile of unopened mail sat on the large walnut desk that had been his father-in-law's. Smythe ignored it. He rummaged through papers and envelopes in a drawer and pulled out a handful of unopened envelopes that he'd sequestered there the day before. He opened them and laid out the bills they contained. He carefully read the numerous charges he'd run up on his credit cards while traveling: hotel suites, chauffeured limousines, lunches and dinners at the fanciest of restaurants, first-class air travel, and gifts from upscale Buenos Aires boutiques. Once he'd begun his multiple trips to Buenos Aires he'd shifted funds into a separate checking account unknown to Cynthia, from which he paid those bills.

He carried them to his pool house office where he wrote checks from a checkbook kept under lock-and-key in a file cabinet, prepared the envelopes for mailing, locked everything up, and slipped the envelopes into his jacket.

He fired up the computer and clicked on the icon labeled 'Franchise.' He spent the next fifteen minutes scrolling through the pages on the screen. When he was finished, he turned off the computer and opened the folder containing Gina's photograph. His groin tingled, and he adjusted himself to accommodate an erection.

It was, he knew, his V-1 time, that moment for pilots when they have used up too much of the runway to abort the takeoff. His flight had already taken off, and there was no returning to earth. The affair with Gina was full-fledged. Commitments had been made. What was lacking was the money he needed to launch his blissful new life with her.

It was time to put into action the business plan he'd been contemplating for a long time.

He was about to become a criminal.

FIVE

Paul Saison was hungover. It wasn't just the wine he'd consumed the night before that caused the pain in his head and the bile in his throat. The donnybrook with Angelique hadn't helped.

The French-Canadian engineer and his live-in girlfriend of the past two years often fought, but last night's fray was particularly nasty. She'd called him a vile, smelly drunk. He countered with, 'You sit on your fat ass all day and do nothing, nothing! *Vieille mégére!*' Being called a vinegary hag really set her off. *'Gorille!'* she screamed, throwing a wine glass at him as she left their apartment, the door slamming so hard the wall shook.

She eventually returned and chose to sleep on the couch rather than curl up next to Saison's hefty, hairy body, and stayed there until he left for work. At Power-Can the next morning he went through the motions of monitoring the plant's electric output on banks of computers. At noon, he informed his supervisor that he had personal matters to attend to and would be late returning from lunch. As far as his boss was concerned, Saison should leave and never come back.

The only thing that kept Saison from being fired was an unstated rule within the company that a certain percentage of engineers, all employees for that matter, were to be French-Canadian to avoid charges of discrimination by the Anglo management. But that didn't mean that men like Saison, who'd worked there eleven years, would ever be promoted – and he hadn't been. He was a fairly skilled engineer, and there had been yearly raises, and an occasional bonus. But from management's perspective, he was lucky to have a job. He was belligerent, cantankerous, odorous, and confrontational, a thoroughly unpleasant man who complained often about his lack of advancement. Twice divorced (there was debate about whether his second marriage had been a legal one), too fond of wine, and with a known gambling addiction, Paul Saison was a liability. His departure would have been cause for celebration at Power-Can.

He drove to the restaurant Carlton Smythe had chosen, Le Papillon, on Church Street. Saison had suggested another place, but Smythe was concerned that he might bump into friends there.

'Hello, Paul,' Smythe said as Saison made

his way to the table his former colleague had commandeered in a quiet, secluded corner.

'Hello, Smythe,' Saison said. He sat and groaned.

'Rough night?'

'*Oui.* That woman, she's driving me crazy.'

Smythe grinned. 'Women can do that,' he said.

'You bet they can. And those *imbéciles* at the plant. You're lucky to be gone.'

'I sometimes think that,' said Smythe. He smiled again. 'How are things at the track? Winning big these days?'

Saison guffawed. 'Winning big? I curse the ponies every day I go to Woodbine.' He was a familiar face at the Toronto race track.

'You should give it up, Paul.'

'Hah! It is in my blood, like a drug, huh? You, Smythe, you look good. All that money you married for. I should find a rich woman and dump that witch I live with.'

'Wine?' Smythe asked.

'Of course.'

Smythe ordered a bottle of French cabernet. Saison told the waiter, 'Pâté, huh? And escargots. We share.' He flashed a smile at Smythe, exposing a missing tooth in his lower jaw. 'Spending some of your wife's money today, huh?'

'And happy to do it, Paul.'

Smythe observed the man across the table who had reported to him at Power-Can during the last few years of Smythe's tenure there as a manager. Most of the food and wine went into Saison's mouth, and he frequently grunted with satisfaction. The French-born Canadian citizen was a large man in every dimension: head, torso, arms and legs. He wore a lightweight, blue and green plaid button-down shirt that needed laundering and that strained at his belly, and khaki pants that could also use a tumble in a washing machine. His face was covered with the beginnings of a scruffy black beard, his greasy black hair pasted to his head with some type of gel.

'So, Smythe,' Saison said after they'd ordered steak for him, a salad for Smythe, 'what's this idea you want to tell me about?'

'It's a what-if situation,' Smythe said.

Saison scrunched up his face in puzzlement. '*Quoi?*'

'Let's say you knew that at precisely nine thirty tonight, all the lights in Toronto were to go out, gone, no electricity. What would you do?'

The big man shrugged. 'Make sure the batteries in my flashlight were good, huh?' He laughed, pleased with his reply.

'No, no, no,' Smythe said. 'I don't mean what you would do to be able to see. Let me be more specific. Tonight, at nine thirty sharp, on the dot, all the electricity in Toronto will go off – and you *know* it's going

51

to go off. And what if you lived next door to a fancy jewelry store filled with diamonds, rubies and emeralds? And let's say, what if you wanted to walk away with some of those jewels, a million dollars worth?'

Saison's eyes widened. He came forward and lowered his voice. 'What the hell are you saying, Smythe? You're going to rob a jewelry store?'

'No, Paul,' Smythe said, 'I'm talking about *you* robbing the store.'

Saison sat back and shook his shaggy head. 'I don't rob stores, Smythe. You know that.' He forced a laugh. 'You're making fun, huh? You like to make fun.'

Now it was Smythe who came forward and spoke softly. 'What I'm asking, Paul, is whether you would pay to know that the power would go off at nine thirty – *if* you wanted to rob the store?'

'Oh. This is like some game, some puzzle, huh? Well, let me see. Hmm. Maybe I would, but—'

'OK,' said Smythe, 'you agree that you would pay for that information.'

'But how would I know before it happens, huh? How would I know the power would be gone, poof, at that time?'

'Because someone will make sure of it.'

'Who?'

Smythe looked down at his half-eaten salad. 'You,' he said quietly.

'*Moi?*'

Smythe nodded.

'Why would I do that?'

'So someone could rob the jewelry store.'

'*Je ne comprends pas.*'

'I'll help you understand, Paul. Just listen to me. And remember, I'm only saying what if? It's a hypothetical situation.'

Smythe had begun his what-if exercise during the massive blackout of 2003 that had plunged much of the nation into darkness. He'd been on a plane about to take off from Vancouver where he'd attended a Power-Can conference when the Air Canada captain announced that they were returning to the gate. 'There's been a blackout that's affecting the eastern part of the country,' he said. 'All flights into Toronto are cancelled until further notice.'

Smythe spent that night in a hotel near the airport. After dinner with other conference attendees, he returned to his room and watched TV coverage of the blackout. His mind wandered as reports from cities up and down the East Coast of the United States, the Mid-West, and the eastern half of Canada played. There was chaos in some places; looting was the big fear, and the police were out in force to prevent it.

What if? Smythe conjured. What if it were possible to *arrange* for a blackout – not a difficult thing to pull off, provided you had an accomplice inside Power-Can – and sell the exact date and time the blackout would occur to someone? Initially, he'd thought in terms of what he'd proffered to Saison, a Toronto jewelry store. But as the months went by and his what-ifs multiplied, his thinking became more grandiose. If one person would pay to know when the power would be shut off to a jewelry store, why not offer the information to others? Find two people willing to pay and allow them to steal from two jewelry stores. Three. Four.

He'd found this fanciful scheme occupying more of his thinking as the years passed, although he'd never intended to put it into action. He was content to have conceived it; it satisfied a need to think in larger terms than what his daily life offered, to think outside the box, something engineers weren't supposed to be good at doing.

But two things happened that caused his flight-of-fancy to take on a more tangible dimension.

The first was meeting a man who was in the business of selling franchises for a chain of fast-food restaurants. He tried to interest Smythe in investing in restaurants in the Toronto area, which Smythe had no intention of doing. But as the salesman extolled the joys of franchising, Smythe found himself thinking not of greasy hamburgers and milk shakes, but how the concept of franchising something valuable – sharing the wealth, as the salesman put it – might fit into his notion of selling blackout dates and times.

The second event that spurred him into action was meeting and falling in love with the beautiful Gina Ellanado.

'I have to get back to the plant,' Saison told Smythe as they topped off their lunch with strong coffee.

'Of course,' Smythe said. 'Thanks for coming and hearing me out.'

Saison looked around the near-empty restaurant before whispering, 'You really want to do this, Smythe?'

'I'm thinking about it, Paul. If I decide to go ahead, are you with me?'

Saison's face sagged into serious thought. 'How much money you say I could make?'

'I'm not sure, but if things were to go right, a quarter-million dollars.'

'Sacrébleu!' Saison's eyes became moist. Despite his overt bravado, he was a sentimental man known to tear up without warning, and without apparent reason.

'Perhaps more,' Smythe said.

As they shook hands on the sidewalk in front of the restaurant, Saison said, 'You know, Smythe, you're a crazy man.'

'No, Paul, I'm not crazy. I'm just—' He

was about to say 'desperate' but swallowed the word. 'This has been between us, not a word to anyone.'

'Of course. You are going to do it?'

'I'm still not certain, Paul, but I needed to know that if I do, you'll be with me.'

Saison slapped his former boss on the arm. 'You *are* a crazy man, Smythe, but you know what?'

'What?'

'Do it!'

SIX

Do it!

Those two words stayed with Smythe as he pulled from the restaurant's parking lot and headed home.

Do it!

Until that day, he'd taken comfort in knowing that he wasn't committed to what had begun as a whimsical bit of daydreaming. But that had changed. He'd made a commitment to Gina that he intended to honor, and that meant money, lots of it. He didn't have funds of his own. Yes, he managed Cynthia's inheritance and could, and had used a portion of it to finance his travels and the free-and-easy lifestyle he enjoyed while on the road. But there was no way he could raid her wealth beyond what he spent to absent himself from her and the house. Old man Wiggins's will, and the pre-nup he'd made Smythe sign prior to marrying 'his little girl,' tied his hands. If he couldn't leave the marriage with big money, *really* big money, there was little sense in doing it. He'd promised Gina a life of opulence and he intended to fulfill that promise. If all went well, they would spend their lives together. That thought filled him with both twitchy joy and anxious dread.

He was terrified that he would lose her if he didn't act quickly. She was the most beautiful and desirable woman in the world. That this delectable creature would commit herself to him, Carlton Smythe, seemed outlandish. But she had made that commitment, and he'd pledged himself to her. Losing her to another man – there must be thousands of more handsome men pursuing her – was a deathly notion. He couldn't allow it to happen.

He stopped at a post office to mail the bills he'd paid, made a second stop at a branch of his bank where he withdrew two thousand dollars in cash, and went to a two-story office building in an industrial area. A large sign announced that it contained fully furnished and serviced office suites for lease. He'd become increasingly nervous about having sensitive materials and Gina's photograph in the pool house, and had decided to find space away from home.

'I'm interested in renting office space for a limited amount of time,' he told the attractive redheaded sales representative.

She replied that there were two spaces available, one large, the other small.

'I don't need much space,' he said. 'I will

need access to the Internet.'

'That's provided,' she said. 'The smaller office will probably be to your liking. Come, I'll show it to you.'

After the tour, he sat across from her as she prepared the rental agreement.

'The name of your company, sir?'

'Ah, it's a one-man consulting business,' he said with a wry smile. 'MAD Enterprises. M-A-D Enterprises.'

'All right,' she said, pointing out that the central phone number that came with the office would be answered in person during normal working hours and by voicemail out-of-hours. 'Any mail will be posted to your box. May I have a credit card for billing purposes?'

'I'd rather not use a card,' he said. 'I'll pay cash in advance.'

She smiled and said that would be fine. Obviously paying in cash was not an unusual situation. He handed her eighteen hundred dollars, enough to pre-pay two months, and left the building fifteen minutes later with a copy of the month-to-month lease, and the keys to the building and his office.

Cynthia was meeting with members of the COC's board when he arrived home. He went upstairs, changed into casual clothing, and walked to the pool house where he loaded Gina's file, and papers he didn't wish discovered, into a briefcase. On his way back to his new hideaway he stopped at an office equipment store and purchased a laptop computer. He cheerfully greeted the redheaded sales rep as he entered the building, went to the leased space, placed the materials in a lockable file cabinet provided by management, and connected the new computer to the Internet.

'I'll be back in a few days with other things,' he told her on his way out, 'a printer and—'

'We provide a printer, fax machine and scanner for our tenants,' she informed him, 'as well as the free use of our conference room – you'll have to reserve it – and secretarial services for a fee.'

'That's good to know,' he said, 'really good to know. I'm looking forward to working here. You have a good day.'

'You too, sir.'

That night over dinner, Cynthia brought up his next trip to Argentina.

'How long will you be gone this time?' she asked, her tone indicating that any answer was unacceptable.

'I'm not sure. It depends on how the meetings go. Four or five days.'

'This has to stop, Carlton.'

'Why are you saying that, Cynthia? It's a business trip.'

'Your business is right here at home, in

Toronto. I want you to give up this ridiculous consulting business of yours.'

'I can't do that.'

'You could if you wanted to.'

'Look, I—'

'Excuse me,' she said, and left him alone at the table.

'Mrs Smythe isn't feeling well?' the housekeeper asked when she came into the dining room and saw that Cynthia had barely touched her dinner.

'That's right,' Smythe answered. 'She has a headache. I have to go out for a while. Sorry to leave such a fine meal, Mrs Kalich.'

The housekeeper's broad, pleasant face creased as she watched him leave. The troubles in the marriage were blatantly clear to her, and she wondered how much longer it would last. She silently sided with Carlton most of the time. Cynthia Smythe could be a difficult woman, terribly spoiled in Mrs Kalich's opinion. Her husband, on the other hand, was a fine man, a mild-mannered and kind gentleman. She hated to see Carlton leave on his business trips. For this housekeeper who'd worked for the family for more than fifteen years, his absences meant having to be alone with Cynthia and her mother, something she did not enjoy.

Smythe drove to a bar twenty minutes away and settled in a corner booth where he ate a cheeseburger and nursed a vodka gimlet. His nerves were on edge. Confrontations with Cynthia were always upsetting, and had become increasingly frequent over the past year. But his domestic situation was the least of it. He'd set into motion this day a grandiose scheme that was, at once, clear to him in its simplicity yet fraught with potential pitfalls.

He was certain that its core idea – that people would pay to know the exact moment in time when there would be a power outage – was sound, and he was confident that arranging for that power shortage was do-able. The problem was identifying and signing up those who would pay for the information.

It was like any other business plan, he thought. You can have the best idea, the best product in the world, but if you don't have paying customers it was all meaningless. He'd given this aspect of the project considerable thought, and felt he might have the answer.

He was well aware that such 'customers' weren't likely to be the nicest of people, and he didn't know such individuals.

Think it out, he silently told himself as he finished his drink, paid his tab, and drove home. *Be smart. You can make it work. You* have *to make it work!*

SEVEN

The Canadian Opera Company's press reception for its upcoming production of *Carmen* was held in the Richard Bradshaw Amphitheatre at the Four Seasons Centre for the Performing Arts, in downtown Toronto. Although most men attending were dressed in business suits, Cynthia had insisted that Carlton wear his tuxedo: 'You are one of the company's representatives,' she explained, 'because you're with me.' She'd bought a new gown for the occasion that looked nice on her in her husband's estimation.

Cast members in costume greeted invited guests as they arrived. Carlton and Cynthia walked in arm-in-arm and joined a knot of familiar faces, which included the production's director who was being interviewed by the opera critic from the *Globe and Mail*. Carlton eavesdropped on their conversation for a few minutes before wandering away in search of the man he'd hoped to see that night, Dominick Martone. He spotted him across the vast room talking with two couples, and sauntered in that direction.

Martone was one of COC's biggest contributors. His business holdings were extensive and wide-reaching, including Canada's largest trash hauling and recycling company, restaurants, clothing and leather goods shops, a printing plant, and an importer of wines and liquors. There was, of course, his 'other business', heading Ontario's leading crime family from which most of his wealth was generated. That he'd never been indicted was testament to his business acumen, as well as to the expensive accountants and attorneys with whom he surrounded himself, to say nothing of having an uncanny talent for financially supporting the right politicians. Of course, those who benefited from his largesse preferred not to believe that he had a dark side. That included myriad charities, performing arts groups like the COC, and other non-profit organizations that had grown dependent upon his generosity. And generous he was, especially where opera was concerned. Those who claimed to know him well spoke of his breaking into tears at the first bars of a favorite aria, although it was doubtful that they broached the subject unless he brought it up. Carlton had once heard him boast that he'd been a baritone at *La Scala* in a previous life.

Smythe stopped short of joining the group

surrounding Martone. He was aware of the two men in suits flanking COC's important benefactor. One was slender with a ferret-like face and an extremely long, crooked nose. The second was a mountain of a man with a shaved head, bulbous facial features, and hands like catchers' mitts. Those who choreographed COC's events knew to include these two additional guests as part of Martone's entourage. They never spoke to anyone as their eyes took in each person who approached, like Secret Service agents protecting heads-of-state. *Bodyguards. Henchmen. Thugs.* Those were the descriptions that formulated in Smythe's mind each time he saw them, men not to be trifled with.

He took in Martone as he always did when in his presence, and had the usual reaction – that he wished he looked like him. The crime family head was compactly built with swarthy skin, large but well-proportioned features, and close-cropped black hair. Too black? Touched up? It didn't matter. His gray, double-breasted pinstripe suit was molded to his body. The physical contrast between Martone and Smythe was unmistakable, Smythe tall and slender, pale, and with silky graying hair, Martone ruggedly handsome, every hair in place, dusky skin, and with large, perfect white teeth rendered especially so against his contrasting complexion.

But there was another aspect of Martone that Smythe envied, which was the man's relaxed demeanor when conversing with others. He seemed to charm everyone he met, chatting easily with them, laughing heartily and making *them* laugh, holding court as though being the center of attention, indeed the universe, was the natural order of things.

Smythe tried to summon the courage to break into the conversation but held back. Having an opportunity to speak with Martone was why he'd accompanied Cynthia that night with more enthusiasm than usual.

As he pondered what to say to allow him to smoothly join them, the other couples, after a final sustained laugh at something Martone had said, drifted away, leaving him momentarily alone.

Smythe moved.

'Ah, Mr Smythe,' Martone said, extending his hand. 'Good to see you again.' His hand was large, his handshake powerful.

'Yes, same here, Mr Martone.'

'Carlton, isn't it?' Martone said. 'I'm Dominick, or Dom if you prefer.'

'Sure. Dom,' Smythe said.

'Where's your lovely wife?'

'Cynthia? She's off somewhere.'

'She's quite a go-getter. The company is fortunate to have her aboard.'

'She loves opera,' Smythe said.

'How can she not? You? Are you an opera buff, too?'

'I like it,' Smythe said, 'although I admit I don't know a lot about it. I'm a good listener.'

Martone slapped Smythe's skinny arm. 'That's what we need, more good listeners to buy tickets.'

Smythe glanced over at one of the two bodyguards, whose eyes were fixated on him. He was tempted to empty his pockets to show that he wasn't armed, a fleeting silly thought. He saw other members of COC's board approaching and knew it was now or never.

'I was hoping to run into you tonight, Dom,' he said quickly. 'I have a—well, I suppose you could call it a business proposition that I'd like to discuss with you.'

Martone's heavy eyebrows went up. 'I'm always willing to talk business,' he said.

They were interrupted by the board members.

Martone said to his big bodyguard, 'Hugo, give Mr Smythe my card.'

Hugo pulled a business card from the lapel pocket of his ill-fitting suit jacket and handed it to Smythe.

'Always happy to speak with a good listener who has a business proposition,' Martone said. 'Give me a call.' He flashed a wide smile, gave Smythe another slap on the arm, and turned to greet the others.

'I will, Dom,' Smythe said. 'Thanks. You'll hear from me.'

He held his breath as he walked away, afraid he'd burst out in a giddy giggle. It had been so easy. Martone hadn't shown skepticism, hadn't summarily dismissed him, hadn't pierced his inner thoughts with his black eyes. They'd spoken as though they were old buddies. He'd slapped him on the arm – twice!

Later that night, after dinner with friends at the 360 Restaurant atop the CN Tower, Carlton and Cynthia returned home. He emptied his tux pockets on the kitchen table before heading upstairs and she spotted Martone's card.

'Why do you have that?' she asked.

'What? Oh, Dom's card? We talked a little business tonight.'

'Business? With Dominick Martone?'

'Yes. I thought that because he has his hand in so many businesses he might have need for a consultant.'

'Carlton,' she said in the tone of a teacher admonishing a student, 'Dominick Martone's businesses don't need an electrical engineer.'

'You're probably right, but I figured nothing ventured, nothing gained. Anyway, he invited me to call him and get together. I know how much you hate my being away so much, and I thought that—'

'That's sweet,' she said, kissing his cheek. 'It would be wonderful if you could find clients closer to home. But Dominick Martone? You know what he *really* does for a living?'

'I've heard the rumors.'

'They're more than rumors,' she said. 'Want to cuddle together tonight?'

'I, ah ... Sure, Cynthia. That would be nice.'

EIGHT

Smythe summoned the courage to call two days later.

'Martone Enterprises,' a woman said.

'Hello. My name is Carlton Smythe. Mr Martone is expecting my call.'

'Oh? Mr Smythe? Can you tell me what this is in reference to?'

'Ah, we had a conversation a few nights ago at the opera house – my wife is on the board – and I mentioned something to Mr Martone and he suggested that I call.'

'Please hold.'

Martone came on the line. 'Hello there,' he said.

'Sorry it took me a few days to get back to you but I've been busy. I was hoping we could get together sometime soon.'

'How's today look for lunch?'

'Today? I, ah, yes, I think I can make that. Yes, lunch today would be fine.'

'Good. Twelve thirty at my restaurant, Martone's, on St Clair Avenue. You know it?'

'Yes, of course. Twelve thirty, you say?'

'See you there, pal.'

Smythe had made the call from his newly-rented office. He sat back, feet up on the desk, and contemplated what he'd put into motion.

To this point, it had been easy, too easy. Now – and the realization caused his stomach to knot – he was about to put into play what had been nothing but a pipedream, a Walter Mitty moment transformed into reality by his love for Gina Ellanado.

He gazed adoringly at her photograph. Buoyed by the fire in her eyes, he again rehearsed the pitch he would make to Dominick Martone.

Toronto has five different areas of the city known informally as 'Little Italy'. Martone's restaurant was located in one of them, west of Bathurst, on St Clair. Smythe had been dispatched to the area a few times by Cynthia when she wanted authentic Italian delicacies for a dinner party, although he'd never stepped foot inside Martone's. He had peered through the window, however, and it appeared to him to be nothing more than a large glorified pizza parlor.

Dressed in what he considered to be his power outfit – navy blue suit, white shirt, and red tie – he arrived a half hour early and strolled along the opposite side of the street from the restaurant, pretending to window shop. At twelve fifteen, a black Town Car pulled up in front of Martone's and its namesake got out, accompanied by the two men often seen with him at public functions. A cold chill struck Smythe. Would they be present at the lunch? If so, did he dare outline his proposal with others listening? He'd have to play that by ear, he decided, as he waited until the three men disappeared into the restaurant.

Smythe checked himself again in a store window. He pulled a cigar from his jacket pocket, clenched it between his teeth, and took another look at himself. Perfect.

At precisely twelve twenty-nine, he crossed the street, drew a deep, prolonged breath, and opened the door. The odor of garlic hit him hard, along with the bright fluorescent lighting and noise level. Most of the Formica tables were occupied, and two middle-aged waitresses scurried among them. A half-dozen people stood at the counter waiting for takeout orders.

Smythe looked for Martone. There was no sign of him, or his colleagues. He wasn't sure what to do, or who to ask. Eventually he went to a man wearing chef's whites who appeared to be in charge. 'Excuse me,' Smythe said, 'I'm looking for Mr Martone.'

The man frowned and looked at Smythe as though he had a smear of tomato sauce on his face. 'He knows you?' he asked.

'Oh, yes. He's expecting me for lunch.'

'What's your name?'

'Smythe. Carlton Smythe.'

The man went to a door at the rear of the restaurant and knocked. After a brief conversation with the Martone bodyguard Smythe now knew was named Hugo, the chef motioned for Smythe. The young, skinny Mafioso and Hugo took in Smythe from head to toe and he wondered whether he would be patted down. They now focused attention on his briefcase. Smythe made a move to open it for inspection but they stepped back to allow him to enter. He took tentative steps into the room where Martone sat at an elaborately-set table for two. The contrast with the pizza parlor area was profound. Subdued lighting was provided by two huge, ornate, gold-leaf chandeliers. The room's carpeting was blood-red. Floor-to-ceiling murals of scenes from popular operas covered the walls. Smythe recognized an aria from Puccini's *Madam Butterfly* oozing from unseen speakers. The men who'd allowed Smythe to enter retreated to a small table in the corner of the room far from their boss.

'Ah, Mr Smythe,' Martone said, getting up and extending his hand. He wore a shiny black suit; the high collar of his white shirt was clearly defined above his jacket. A gray silk tie was neatly knotted and secured to his shirt with a diamond tie tack. Black patent leather shoes with tassels completed the Mafioso's ensemble.

'Right on time,' he said. 'I like that in a businessman. Sit down, sit down. Be comfortable.' He said to one of his bodyguards, 'Tell Paulie to get in here.'

Paulie, the man in whites who'd directed Smythe to where Martone waited, appeared in the doorway. Martone looked at Smythe. 'Red, white, a beer, whiskey?'

'Whatever you're having is fine,' Smythe replied.

'A bottle of red,' Martone told Paulie, 'and an antipasto platter, hot. So,' he said to Smythe, 'what did you think of *Carmen* the other night?'

'Oh, I liked it a lot. Very fine performance.'

'I thought the soprano was weak on the Habanera. Other than that, I thought it was pretty good.' He sat back, hands folded on his midsection, closed his eyes, and said, almost sang, 'Love is a rebellious bird that no one can tame.' His eyes opened. 'I love that line, huh? So true. What about you, Smythe? How's your love life?'

Smythe was startled by the question. He fumbled before saying, 'Pretty good ... Dom.'

'Good to hear. You've been married a long time, huh?'

'Thirty years.' He wondered whether Martone expected him to talk about his mistresses. Instead, the mob boss said, 'I believe in marriage, Smythe. Family!' He slapped his hand on the table. 'Family is everything!'

'I agree,' Smythe said, realizing that his unlit cigar was still wedged between his teeth.

'You smoke those things?' Martone asked, grimacing. 'Not good for you. I gave 'em up years ago.'

'I just have a ... well, I'm about to give up the habit, too.' He removed the cigar from his mouth and shoved it into the breast pocket of his suit jacket.

Paulie arrived with the wine and platter of hot antipasto. He poured the wine into the two glasses on the table and asked if Martone wanted to order lunch.

'In a minute,' Martone said, waving his hand. 'We've got business to discuss.'

The mob boss raised his glass in Smythe's direction. Smythe returned the gesture.

'So, pal, what's this business you want to talk to me about?'

Smythe's nerves had been on edge since leaving the house. It had been so unexpectedly easy to set up the meeting with Martone, a casual chat at the opera and a short, simple phone call. But this was the moment of truth. Smythe's biggest problem in rehearsing for the meeting was how to broach the subject of offering a criminal proposal without indicating that he knew that Martone was not only a criminal, but was also the head of a powerful crime syndicate. After all, the man didn't hand out business cards with 'Mafia Boss' printed on them. He'd established himself in eastern Canada as a prosperous businessman and patron of the arts. Most people knew, of course, about his connection with organized crime but were willing to ignore that in return for his largesse. Now, Smythe was about to say in effect, *I know that you're a Mafioso, Mr Martone, and here's another way for you to add to your illegal fortune.*

He'd been grappling with that all morning and hadn't come to a satisfactory conclusion, hadn't formulated the right way to put it. But as he sat across from the smiling Martone a sense of wellbeing and confidence swept over him. He'd come to the restaurant with a solid proposal, one that could conceivably earn Martone's crime family millions of dollars. With Gina's smiling face hovering over the table, he pulled the cigar from his pocket, clenched it between his teeth, sat back, crossed one leg over the other, and said in a well-modulated voice, 'I'm here to offer you a franchise.'

Martone came forward, his smile a memory. 'What is this franchise thing?' he asked. 'Some chicken shack or pizza joint? I've got all the pizza I can eat.' He used his hand to indicate where they were. 'You want to sell me a *franchise*?'

Smythe nodded and widened his smile. 'No chicken, no pizza, Dom,' he said. 'This is a brand-new franchise idea that'll make you millions.'

Martone shrugged and sat back, flipped a hand in the air. 'Go ahead, pal, tell me about this million-dollar franchise idea of yours. But make it short, OK? Get to the point. I'm hungry.'

Smythe drew a breath and said, 'It's simple, Dom. I can offer you a date, time and place.'

'Yeah? That doesn't sound too exciting, Smythe.'

'Oh, but it can be ... Dom.'

'What are you talking about?'

'A date, time and place: when the entire eastern seaboard will be without electricity – everything black up and down the coast and here in Canada. Precise. You can set your watch by it. Simple and clean, the way I'm sure you prefer your business deals.'

Smythe sensed that Martone was beginning to lose patience and decided to be more direct. 'OK,' he said, 'let me lay it out for you in simple terms. I tell you when all power will go off up and down the east coast and here in Canada. You can use that knowledge any way you wish – here in Toronto. I'll be selling that same information to others like you.' He paused to see whether Martone took offense at being lumped in with others. He didn't seem to be, so he continued. 'That's why I call it a franchise. Everybody who pays me for the information receives his own exclusive franchise for a particular part of the affected area. What they do with the information is their business. The same goes for you.'

It started as a low rumble before turning into a full-fledged belly laugh, which annoyed Smythe. He felt as though he was being laughed at, dismissed as someone who'd arrived with a bad joke. Martone sensed his reaction. He held up his hand as he brought his laughter under control. 'Hey, no offense, pal, but what you're telling me is ... well, it's different, huh? I mean, I've been in business a long time but I never heard of anything like this.'

As suddenly as the laugh had erupted, it vanished, replaced by a hard stare from the Mafioso. He pointed his index finger at Smythe and said, 'What you're telling me sounds like it's not legit, you know, dishonest, not kosher. I'm a legitimate businessman, Smythe, always above board, no games. How do you expect me to react to this – what's the term the Jews use, cockamamie? – this cockamamie scheme you've come up with.'

'I shouldn't have wasted your time,'

Smythe said, picking up his briefcase from the floor and standing.

'Hey, hey, hey, calm down, my friend. Like I said, no offense. Sit down. We'll eat a good meal and maybe it'll help me digest this thing you're talking about. We digest a good meal and then I digest this franchise thing.'

It occurred to Smythe that it would be wise to make amends with Martone, or at least to not upset him. He wielded considerable power with the opera company. To alienate him wouldn't be fair to Cynthia – or taken lightly by her.

'Sure, Dom,' Smythe said, glancing at Martone's two bodyguards who seemed disinterested in what was going on at their boss's table. He resumed his seat and flashed a smile at Martone. 'I know that what I'm offering sounds a little farfetched, Dom, but not only will it work, it'll generate millions for anybody who signs on.'

Martone ignored the comment, called for Paulie, and ordered for both. 'We'll have the veal parm,' he said. 'The veal nice and thin, and tender.'

'Oh, yeah, Mr Martone.'

'Ziti on the side, red sauce, and salads, house dressing.' To Smythe: 'Another bottle of red?'

'No, thanks, I think not.'

'Good for you. Keep the mind sharp. So, let's talk opera.'

An hour later they shook hands as Smythe prepared to leave.

'Thanks for your time and for hearing me out,' Smythe said.

'Hey, I'm always interested in new ideas. You just pitched it to the wrong guy.' He leaned close to Smythe's ear. 'I'm gonna forget that you thought I might be interested in something illegal, Smythe. It stays right here in this room, huh?'

'Of course.' Smythe opened his briefcase and took out a file folder containing copies of the charts he'd created that spelled out the potential return on an investment in his franchise. He handed it to Martone. 'I'll leave this with you, Dom. I know you're not interested in what I'm offering but maybe you'll find the numbers interesting.'

'Yeah, sure. Thanks. See you at the next production.'

Smythe was happy to be gone from the room and from under Martone's looming presence. At the same time he left with a strange, undefined sense that it hadn't been a wasted lunch. For some reason he thought that despite the Toronto crime boss's initial displeasure with the project, he hadn't totally dismissed it.

He was right.

Martone called the following afternoon.

NINE

'Smythe, Dom Martone here. Tomorrow morning, eleven sharp. Take the ferry over to the islands. We meet at the Franklin Children's Garden, Pine Grove, by the Franklin-the-Turtle sculpture. Got it?'

'By the—?'

'Eleven sharp. Dress casual. *Ciao!*'

Smythe hastily scribbled on a pad what he remembered of Martone's instructions. *Meet at the Children's Garden? Dress casual?* Was the Mafioso joking? Couldn't be. One thing was certain. Martone hadn't set up the meeting to dismiss Smythe's franchise idea. He was obviously interested.

But despite this positive sign Smythe was gripped with conflicting emotions.

Martone's parting comment after lunch the previous day – 'I'm gonna forget that you thought I might be interested in something illegal' – stayed with him. He'd basically accused the Mafioso of being just that, a thug, someone who dealt in illegalities, and wondered whether Martone would want him dead once the deal was finalized, put a hit on him in gangster parlance, send him to sleep with the fishes.

But if that was Martone's intention it wasn't about to happen that day. The Mafioso wouldn't plan an execution in the middle of a kids' playground. He would have suggested a night meeting at some abandoned warehouse along the waterfront.

Eleven in the morning? The Children's Garden? Lots of dirty little ones racing around while their mothers looked on adoringly? Then Smythe had a revelation and smiled at the conclusion to which he'd come. This Dominick Martone was one clever guy. Who would ever guess that he was meeting in a children's playground to discuss a major criminal undertaking? *Don't underestimate him*, Smythe reminded himself. *Don't get cocky. Keep your cool and stand your ground.*

Content that he hadn't been summoned to his own murder, Smythe left the office and swung by their travel agent's office to pick up his airline ticket for the next trip to Buenos Aires. He was scheduled to leave in three days, which put on the pressure. He not only had to suffer three days of Cynthia's complaints about his being away again, he felt the need to close the deal, to be able to tell Gina that he would soon be worth millions and free to spend the rest of his life with her.

It was a lovely sunny day in Toronto the following morning, the sky blue, the temperature moderate. Smythe hadn't slept well and was up far in advance of his alarm's buzz. Cynthia was still in bed when he left the house. He drove to a municipal parking garage near the ferry terminal on Queen's Quay, between Bay and Yonge Streets. He'd heeded Martone's order to dress casually. He chose tan slacks, a blue button-down shirt, a lightweight yellow V-neck sweater and coffee loafers sans socks. He'd had the feeling during lunch with Martone that the Mafioso disapproved of the length of his hair and had considered getting a haircut, but ran out of time.

He boarded the next departing boat and arrived on Toronto Islands more than an hour early for the meeting. He passed the time at the lakeside until his watch said ten fifty-five. It took only a few minutes to walk to the Children's Garden where he saw Martone standing next to the Franklin-the-Turtle sculpture, based upon the Paulette Bourgeois children's book of the same name. Martone had abandoned his suit for a pair of jeans, a white cable-knit sweater draped over his shoulders preppy-style, a pink shirt, and sneakers. He looked out of place in the playground, but Smythe reasoned that if you didn't know what Martone did for a living you wouldn't come to that conclusion. Hugo sat on a bench and glared.

The Mafioso waved to Smythe to join him. Martone nudged Smythe in the arm with his elbow and pointed to a boy of about six or seven who ran in circles around a bear sculpture. A young woman, whom Smythe assumed was the nanny, stood near him.

'He's a real pistol, huh?' Martone said.

'Who? That kid?'

'My grandson, Dominick. Named after me.'

Had Martone invited him there to admire his grandson? He answered his own question. Having his grandson with him gave cover.

'He's cute,' Smythe said.

'Full of piss-and-vinegar like his grandfather. Let's take a walk.'

'You can leave him alone?'

'He's got the nanny with him. Come on. We've got things to discuss.'

They found a bench a hundred yards from where the child played. 'Like I told you at lunch, Smythe, I needed to digest this thing you're talking about.'

Smythe drew a breath and waited.

'So I did. Digest it. Gave me heartburn.' He laughed. 'A couple of Tums took care of it. So, I digested it and made a decision.'

Smythe maintained his silence.

'The way I figure it,' Martone said, 'this

scheme of yours is no different than insider trading on the stock market, like knowing when a company's about to buy another because you're an insider and you tell your friends about it and they buy the stock of the company being taken over. I mean, all I'm getting from you is a date and time, which I pass on to somebody else. Am I correct?'

'I hadn't thought of it in those terms, Dom, but you make sense. Of course in this case I *sell* that information to someone else.'

'So I'm maybe interested in going in on it. You want a partner, right?'

'Ah ... yes, I suppose that's what I'm looking for. A few partners.'

'I've had a lot of partners, Smythe. Sometimes it works out, sometimes it doesn't. You come off to me like a straight-shooter. Am I wrong?'

'If you mean can I be trusted, the answer is no, you're not wrong.'

'Good, good. But I've got a problem with this.'

'Oh?'

'See, you tell me that you'll take me in as a partner for Toronto, but that you'll look for other partners in other places.'

Smythe nodded.

'The problem, Smythe, is that you don't know the sort of businessmen who might be interested in getting involved.'

He was right. Smythe had launched his plan with someone he already knew through Cynthia's involvement with the opera company. He had no idea who he might approach next in different cities, and had realized from the beginning that this represented a potential flaw, a big one. What Martone said next was music to his ears.

'Here's what I'm suggesting, Smythe. I know lots of people who might want to buy what you call a franchise. They're friends of mine. You might say we're in the same business.'

He didn't have to spell it out. He was talking about other Mafia bosses.

'The way I see it, Smythe, you need me for more than just Toronto. You need me as a full partner, somebody who can reach the right people with the right kind of money to invest. You follow?'

'I follow, Dom.'

'The question is, how do we put together this partnership of ours? What do you want out of it? Fifty-fifty?'

Smythe hadn't prepared for this sort of conversation. He'd made numerous projections on his computer about how much the scheme might generate, but it was all predicated on identifying and selling a dozen or more franchises to mob leaders in other cities. Martone was right. Making contact and selling the idea to other Mafioso was daunting at best.

How much did Smythe want?

He pulled numbers out of a hat.

'A million for the information, Dom.' He added as an afterthought, 'And a piece of the action over a million.'

'A million from me,' Martone said. 'You want a million just to sell me the info?'

'If that's too steep I can—'

Martone patted his arm, like a father comforting a son who's gotten involved with the wrong girl. 'Here's the deal, Smythe. I give it to you once, just once. You take it or we never discuss it again. *Capisce?*'

'Yes.'

'We become partners,' Martone said. 'I pay you a million bucks, half upfront, half after the deal is done. I sell the franchises to my friends and keep the first two million. After that we split, seventy-thirty, seventy to me, thirty per cent to you. How's that sound?'

'It sounds good, Dom, but I need expense money, too.'

'Whoa, what are you saying? What expenses?'

'It'll cost me money to pull this off, to create the blackout.'

'You can't cover it out of the million?'

'I could,' Smythe said, hoping he hadn't made a tactical error by asking for more, 'but I need to clear a million dollars. I need another two hundred and fifty thousand on top of the million.' Martone's facial expression didn't indicate that he was about to balk, so Smythe decided to go for broke. 'How about this?' he said. 'I need money in advance for another business deal I'm pursuing. Give me a million, two hundred and fifty thousand and you can keep all the proceeds after that.'

Did I blow the deal? he wondered.

'You strike a harder bargain than you look, Smythe. OK. You've got a deal.'

Martone extended his hand. Smythe took it. 'To me, Smythe, a handshake is as good as any legal paper any lawyer could draw up.' He looked at Smythe with cold, coal-black eyes. 'Now,' he said, 'give me the info.'

'What?'

'The info. The date, time, whatever.'

'Wait a minute, Dom, why should I give it to you before I get paid?'

'You don't trust me?'

'You don't trust *me*?' Smythe countered.

Martone paused, then laughed.

Smythe returned it with a smile. A pervasive sense of control came over him. He met Martone's stare, unflinching, challenging.

'OK,' Martone said. 'We arrange for the swap, the money for you, the info for me. Tomorrow?'

'No. I need more time to put things into

place.'

'How much time?'

'I'll be out of town for a few days. I need ... I need three weeks. It's not easy to set this thing up.' He fought to contain his glee at how easily things had fallen into place, and decided to press the money issue. 'I need some start-up funds, Dom. Can you advance me a couple of hundred thousand against the million two-fifty?'

Martone laughed. 'I figured you'd want some seed money, Smythe.' He motioned to Hugo, who left the bench and came to his boss's side. 'Give him the envelope,' Martone said. Hugo handed Smythe a thick number ten envelope and walked away.

'There's fifty Gs in there,' Martone told Smythe. 'I'll deduct it from what we agreed on.'

'Thanks, Dom,' Smythe said as Martone's grandson threw himself into his grandfather's arms.

'Hey, big guy, easy, easy. Say hello to Mr Smythe.'

The boy grimaced and stuck out his tongue at Smythe. 'You suck,' he said.

Martone put the kid on the ground and delivered a sharp slap to his rear end. 'Hey, I told you, you don't talk fresh,' he said.

His grandson burst into tears and ran back to where the nanny now sat with Hugo.

'Kids,' Martone said. 'They don't learn respect these days. You go ahead, Smythe, leave. I'll stay awhile with the kid.'

Smythe walked away, a smile on his face. It was falling into place. He'd have a million dollars to take to Buenos Aires and enough to pay Saison.

Now all he had to do was decide what that date would be, and that meant meeting again with the big French-Canadian.

TEN

Smythe was told when he called Power-Can that Saison had taken a personal day off. The Frenchman answered the phone at home.

'Hung over?' Smythe asked pleasantly.

'Too much wine, too much of the bitch. What do you want?'

'We need to talk.'

'So go ahead and talk.'

'Not on the phone. I assume Angelique isn't there?'

'Gone to work. She should stay away.'

'Pull yourself together, Paul. I'll be there in an hour.'

Saison's apartment was a third-floor walk-up. The pungent odor of cooking, wine, and cigarette and cigar smoke greeted Smythe as he ascended the stairs. He found the aroma pleasant. Cynthia had an obsession about odors and their home smelled antiseptic, as though constructed of HEPA filters. Elaborate air-cleaning machines housed in decorative wood shells silently cleansed the air in every room.

Saison answered Smythe's knock. He looked as bad as he'd sounded on the phone. Smythe's call had obviously wakened him. His hair went in a dozen different directions and he hadn't shaved in days. He wore a stained white sleeveless undershirt, red boxer shorts, and sandals. His eyes mirrored his pain. Smythe declined an offer of a drink and sat at the small table in the kitchen. The sink overflowed with dirty dishes; a skinny black-and-white cat slept soundly in sun streaming through the window.

'You remember that thing we talked about at lunch?' Smythe asked.

Saison rubbed his eyes and yawned. 'That crazy idea of yours?'

'Right, that crazy idea of mine. It's not just a crazy idea any more, Paul. I'm going to do it.'

'You're going to do it?'

'You told me to do it. I'm doing it – with you.'

'Oh, I don't know, Smythe.'

Smythe stared at him. 'You're backing out?'

'No, no, but I thought maybe you were kidding, like daydreaming.'

'It started as a daydream but now it's about to become a reality. Maybe I was wrong to think that you agreed to be part of it. I thought you wanted the money but it looks like I was wrong.'

Smythe stood.

'No, Smythe, sit down. I'm, ah, I'm just waking up, you know, a little fuzzy. Tell me again about this idea of yours.'

Smythe slowly and carefully outlined the plan. At a specified day and time Saison was to create a glitch in Power-Can's generators. This disruption needed to last only a few seconds before the power company's antiquated mechanical switches, overwhelmed by the power surge, began to shut down the grid that provided power from Toronto southward and westward, cutting off the flow of electricity to Chicago and Cleveland, Buffalo, Boston, New York, Washington DC, and Baltimore. The sudden blackness would be instantaneous. Smythe estimated that it would take a minimum of six hours for engineers up and down the grid to trace the cause back to the Power-Can plant, probably longer if past blackouts were any gauge.

'Make sense?' Smythe asked when he'd finished going over the plan.

Saison had listened intently, his only interruptions an occasional belch or grunt. He got up from the table, went to the kitchen, and returned with a bottle of French table wine and two glasses. Smythe watched with amusement as Saison filled both glasses and handed one to him. 'How much you say for me?' Saison asked.

'That depends on how many franchises I

can sell,' Smythe lied.

On his way there he'd considered giving Saison a lower figure than the quarter of a million dollars he'd originally offered. The drunken Frenchman would probably be happy with half that amount. But Smythe also knew that as much as he found the Frenchman personally offensive, he needed him. Everything depended upon having someone inside Power-Can with enough knowledge of the complex electrical system to cause the blackout.

There was another dimension to Smythe's thought process regarding money. Now that he had a commitment from Martone for a million, two hundred fifty thousand, he'd begun to question whether it was enough to finance his escape to Argentina and to support the sort of lifestyle Gina would expect. Every additional dollar he could squeeze out of the deal would be that much more he had to finance the luxurious lifestyle he envisioned for himself and his lovely Argentinean lover.

'A hundred thousand,' Smythe said.

Saison glared at him. 'You said more, a quarter of a million.'

'That was before I made my deal with the money man, Paul. He cut down on what I get, so I have to pay you less.' Saison started to protest but Smythe added, 'Hey, Paul, when was the last time you saw a hundred thousand dollars in cash? Think about it. You can pay your debts, dump Angelique, and find a new and better place to live.'

Saison growled and pouted.

'All right,' Saison said, 'I'll make it a hundred and twenty-five thousand. All cash, upfront, in your pocket. That's a good payday for tripping a couple of switches.'

Another grunt from Saison.

'OK,' Smythe said, 'I'll sweeten the deal. The money man is paying me a percentage of the profits once they reach a certain level. Between you and me, Paul, I plan on leaving Toronto once the blackout occurs. You can have my percentage of the profits.'

'How do I get that?'

'I'll tell the money man who you are and have him pay my share to you.'

'Where are you going?'

'That's a secret.'

'You're leaving your wife?'

'Let's just say that I'll be starting a new life. Enough talk. Do we have a deal or don't we?'

Saison brought his glass down on the table with enough force to cause half its contents to spill over the top. 'No, Smythe. You said a quarter of a million. You want me to put my neck on the line for less? No deal, Smythe. What good is what you say this money man will give me after it's over? You think you're the only one who'll take off, be gone? You think I'd be stupid enough to stay around. I'm not stupid, Smythe. You give me what you promised or you find somebody else for this crazy plan.'

Two things crossed Smythe's mind at that moment.

The first was what he knew from the beginning that without someone like Saison inside Power-Can there would be no blackout. He knew others who worked there but none of them were likely to go along with the scheme. Saison's discontent with Power-Can – with almost everything for that matter – and his perpetual state of being broke due to his gambling habit, gave him the right incentive. Two: Saison now knew of Smythe's intentions. If he became disgruntled enough he might decide to tell someone at Power-Can of the plot.

'You drive a hard bargain, Paul,' Smythe said through an exaggerated sigh. 'All right. A quarter of a million it is.'

'What about the piece of the action from the money man?'

'That, too.' Agreeing to that was easy. Smythe would be long gone before it became an issue.

Saison replaced what had spilled from his glass and raised it to Smythe. 'You're a crazy man, Smythe, really crazy. But so am I, *oui*? Here's to becoming rich. *A votre santé*, Smythe. Cheers!'

ELEVEN

Two days later, Smythe boarded a flight to Buenos Aires. Cynthia had complained about his taking another trip, and her mother weighed in, too, but Smythe kept his cool and avoided an outright argument with either woman.

Prior to leaving he'd taken the bills Martone had given him and divided them into groups of ten. Twenty thousand dollars was stashed in a small safe he'd purchased which he'd secured beneath his desk in the rented office. He put ten of the bills in his wallet and separated the remaining twenty thousand into two batches, each wrapped in clothing in the suitcase he'd be using for the trip. He knew that he was taking a chance on airport security personnel deciding to go through the suitcase but didn't see any other option. He'd never been singled out before at the airport, nor had Customs officials in Buenos Aires red-flagged him for a more thorough examination. He always dressed nicely for the flights, and his non-descript appearance, along with official-looking but out-of-date correspondence from the Argentine power authority inviting him to make a presentation meant that he'd never had any trouble. He knew that in the future he'd have to make other arrangements, but for now he would take his chances.

He'd sailed through security at JFK Airport, and was asked only a few cursory questions by Customs in Buenos Aires before being waved through. He'd instructed Gina to hire a car service and to meet his flight, which she did.

Seeing her waiting for him as he walked off the flight sent his heart racing. They engaged in a long embrace and sensuous kiss, much to the delight of other passengers, and were soon on their way to the Four Seasons Hotel where Smythe had reserved his usual executive suite. He couldn't keep his hands off her during the ride, causing her to giggle and to push him away, indicating the driver as her reason for warding off his advances. 'Later,' she cooed, 'later.'

But once ensconced in the suite, she welcomed his pent-up passion and they made love, first on the bed, and then when Smythe insisted that they throw caution to the wind, on a chaise longue on the balcony.

Back inside, Gina stood naked in front of a full-length mirror and complained that she was gaining weight. Smythe came up behind her and kneaded the modest roll of her belly. 'I love every inch of you, *mi angel de amor*. I worship every inch of my Gina.'

They dressed and ordered room service. The waiter uncorked a bottle of 2004 Noeima de Patagoina, the most expensive red on the wine list, and poured two glasses before backing from the room. Smythe raised his glass to Gina and said, 'To my wife soon to be, Mrs Carlton Smythe.' With that, he opened his suitcase, extracted the twenty thousand dollars in cash and tossed the bills into the air above her head.

'What is this?' she asked gleefully, snatching bills as they floated down.

'The beginning of our new life together,' Smythe said. 'Listen to me, Gina. I have brought with me twenty thousand dollars US. At today's exchange rate that is more than one hundred thirty thousand Argentine pesos.'

'You bring it with you on the plane?'

'Yes. I brought it for you – for us. I must return home in a few days, but while I am gone I want you to find us a lovely home to rent in which we can live as man and wife, something in a pretty area with nice views, vistas, *si*? Maybe you can find something on a lake or a river, or the ocean. It must be on a hill and have large windows, very large windows to shine light on you. Later we will buy a home together.'

'You want me to do this?'

'Yes. This money is only a small amount. But I will eventually bring for us a large amount of money, a million dollars.'

Her already large brown eyes widened. 'A million dollars?'

'Yes. *Si*. I have been reading about buying property here in Argentina. The right real estate agent will not ask questions about where you have gotten the money.'

'I have a friend in real estate,' she said. 'I will call him.'

'Good. We will also need a bank in which I can deposit funds. Take some of this twenty thousand dollars and open a joint checking account in both our names.'

She nodded and touched his hand. 'I have a friend,' she said, 'who is president of a small bank here in Buenos Aires, a private bank.'

'"Private bank?"'

'Yes. He will do what I say.'

'Good,' Smythe said, wondering how close she was to these 'friends' and wishing they weren't men. The thought of her being intimate with another man was excruciating.

'I will come back with the million dollars. We will use what we must to purchase our dream house, and will have the rest to live together in bliss, sheer bliss. Do you understand?'

She nodded, but then pouted. 'You have

your divorce?'

'Not yet, but it's in the works.'

What was 'in the works' was the scenario that Smythe had concocted regarding Cynthia. The way he'd figured it, once he'd left the country Cynthia would naturally file for divorce, which he would easily grant from Argentina. The fury that his escape would fuel in her – and in her mother – wasn't pleasant to contemplate, but he would be far enough away to not suffer the brunt of it.

'You will do it?' he asked Gina.

'Yes, I will do it.' She broke into a long, hearty laugh, threw herself onto his lap, and kissed him. 'You are a crazy man, Carlton Smythe, *loco, muy loco.*'

'And I am a man madly in love with Gina Ellanado. Let's go out and celebrate, the best restaurant, the best wines, and if you wish we will tango into the wee hours.'

While Smythe laid out his plans for Gina and their life together in Argentina, a conversation of a different sort was taking place in Toronto, Canada.

'I can't believe that you're saying this, Mother,' Cynthia Smythe said. 'Carlton having an affair? That's preposterous. Carlton is not the sort of man who would do that. I mean, look at him. He's hardly what you would call a lady killer, a Casanova.'

Mrs Wiggins bestowed upon her only

child a condescending smile that mirrored what she was thinking, that her daughter was naïve and not terribly bright.

'You must trust me, dear,' she said sweetly. 'I have only your best interests at heart. I might also tell you that I speak from experience.'

It took Cynthia a moment to process what her mother was saying. 'What experience?'

Mrs Wiggins sighed deeply and played with her wedding ring which she'd never removed after her husband's death. 'I've never told this to anyone, Cynthia, but I feel that considering what you are going through it's my duty to be straightforward in the hope that it will bring you to your senses. I shall be blunt. Your father had an affair during our marriage.'

'No!'

'Oh yes, my dear. Your father was – well, let me just say that he succumbed to what most men do, what the psychologists and psychiatrists call a "mid-life crisis". You know what I mean. They see less hair on their heads, and their waistlines expand along with their egos. They feel the need to reassert their masculinity by attracting a different woman than the one to whom they are married and have pledged life-long fidelity. It's very sad really, truly tragic, but it is built into their genetic make-up I fear.'

'*Daddy* had an affair?'

'Yes, he certainly did, with a floozy who worked in one of his offices, one of those young women lacking any sense of morality but certainly not lacking obvious feminine charms. Your father took up with her on a business trip; he took so many business trips that I suppose the temptation was too great for him to overcome, like that salesman Willy Loman in the play.'

'What was her name?' Cynthia asked.

Mrs Wiggins waved away the question. 'It doesn't matter. What *does* matter is that she enticed your father into a compromising position in some hotel room, and continued until I put a stop to it.'

'You confronted Daddy about it?'

'Oh, did I ever. When I began to suspect that his business trips involved more than business, monkey business, I hired a private investigator.'

'You didn't!'

'Of course I did. My honor was at stake, as well as my marriage.'

'Why didn't you leave him? I would leave Carlton if I found out that he was seeing another woman.'

Another patronizing smile from her mother. 'My dear, sweet Cynthia, you have such a romantic view of marriage, which is fine when you're younger, but hardly practical after the years pass by. I was not about to leave your father and the pleasant lifestyle he'd provided for me. I'm no fool, Cynthia.'

'But you said you'd confronted him.'

'That's right, I did, once I had the report and the photographs from the private investigator. I laid them on the table and said nothing, simply waited to hear what he had to say in defense of himself.'

'Did he ... defend himself?'

'He tried. When he was finished jabbering away like a schoolchild caught with his fingers in the cookie jar, I took the report and photographs, tore them in half, and tossed them into the fireplace.'

'That was it?'

'Yes, aside from telling your father that if he ever strayed again I would personally tear out his eyeballs with my fingernails, and take pleasure in doing it.'

Cynthia winced at the visual.

'And so, my dear, my instincts tell me that your husband with all his so-called business trips is seeing another woman. I feel it in my bones, and my bones never lie to me.'

There was nothing for Cynthia to do but cry.

Mrs Wiggins ignored her daughter's tears and said, 'I've already contacted the son of the private investigator who handled my case. His father, dear soul, is no longer with us, but his son is equally capable, I'm sure. I'd like you to think seriously about this overnight, Cynthia. Once you've overcome your natural reluctance to believe that your husband is cheating on you, I'll put you in touch with him.'

Cynthia spent a sleepless night picturing Carlton in bed with another woman. By the time she arose the following morning she'd made her decision.

'I want to meet with the investigator, Mother. I want to do it as soon as possible.'

'I knew that you'd come to that conclusion, Cynthia. But I must give you a very important word of warning. Until the investigator has done his job and reported his results, you must not let Carlton know of your suspicions, not a word. He must be oblivious to it. Do you understand?'

'Yes, Mother.'

'Good girl. I've noticed that some of your clothing is out-of-date. What I suggest is that we go on a shopping spree, mother and daughter, like we used to.'

'That sounds wonderful,' Cynthia said. 'Thank you. I don't know what I'd do without you.'

TWELVE

Smythe was a bundle of nerves when he left Buenos Aires and flew back to Toronto. He'd managed to mask it from Gina, but once on the plane a sense of dread that had been building came out in full flower for this formerly law-abiding, mild-mannered, peace-loving, pocket-protected engineer.

He'd tried to calm his nerves by drinking more than he usually did on a flight, and applying a slide-rule approach to problem-solving. He was minimally successful on both counts.

Since the moment that Dominick Martone had agreed to the scheme, Smythe had been haunted by the question of why the Mafioso chief would agree to turn over a million dollars to a man he barely knew, and without any written agreement. The answer was obvious of course. You don't draw up contracts for a criminal enterprise. Besides, Martone didn't need a written agreement or a lawyer to protect his million dollar investment. He had Hugo and a hundred other

106

Hugos to make sure that Smythe held up his end of the bargain. *Bargain!* He'd made a pact with the Devil, and even if he wanted to back out of the deal he knew that it was too late.

He was also increasingly concerned that the people Martone would recruit to pay for information about the blackout would not hesitate to hurt others if necessary, and made a mental note to insist to Martone the next time they met that no one be injured, at least not physically.

The possibility of going to Martone, returning his money, and saying, 'I changed my mind' came and went, but Smythe knew that he could never abandon the project. What Martone's response would be was grim enough. But he was doing it for Gina, and the thought of losing her was more frightening than broken kneecaps, pulled fingernails, and decapitation-by-chainsaw.

Who were these other men that she knew, the real estate agent and the banker? Were they former lovers? *Current* lovers? He groaned at the thought and decided that he had to speed up the process, shorten the time it would take to leave Toronto with a million dollars and begin life anew with his Gina, his *belleza delirante*, his *deseo de mi corazon*: terms of endearment he'd learned from his Spanish-English dictionary.

His arrival home was surprisingly warm.

Cynthia kissed him with more passion than she had in years, and asked whether his trip had been pleasant and successful.

'Successful, yes,' he said. 'Pleasant? My client seems to think that he owns me, demands my presence day and night.'

'Oh, poor dear,' she said. 'I'll make us a drink.'

'No, I'll make them,' he said.

'Absolutely not,' she said. 'You always put too much vermouth in my martinis, but I'll make yours just the way you like it.' Smythe's martini-making skill was one of many sources of conflict between them. No matter how little vermouth he put in hers it was always too much. Once, he didn't put any vermouth in her drink and she still complained. When he told her what he'd done she refused to believe him.

'Here's to having you home, Carlton,' Cynthia said, raising her glass.

'Thanks,' he said.

'My pleasure,' she said through a sweet smile.

Smythe stayed at the house his first day and evening back in Toronto as a gesture to Cynthia, although he was anxious to get to his rented office where he could think more clearly. The next afternoon he said he needed to meet with a potential Toronto client and would be having dinner with him. Cynthia said that was fine; she was having dinner with board members from the opera company. Her demeanor hadn't changed. She was unfailingly pleasant, even loving, and told him that she was pleased he was seeking clients who wouldn't involve as much overseas travel. 'It's too much wear-and-tear on my honey,' she said.

Smythe went to his rented office the next day and called Paul Saison at Power-Can. 'Can you talk?'

'Sure I can talk. What do you think I am, Smythe, stupid? I went to school, didn't I?'

Smythe ignored the Frenchman's hearty laugh and said, 'We have to get together. What time do you get off?'

'An hour, not soon enough.'

Saison suggested meeting at a bar in which he hung out but Smythe nixed it. 'It's too close to Power-Can,' he said.

'Close is good,' said Saison. 'The *salope* has the car. The witch. She goes to visit her worthless sister.'

'How were you going to get home?'

'The way I came to work, huh? The taxi.'

'We'll go someplace away from the plant.'

'Whatever you say, Smythe.'

'I'll meet you at the corner where that Chinese restaurant is, you know, in that small shopping center?'

'That's six blocks, Smythe. Long walk.'

'And far enough away from the plant,' Smythe said, and hung up.

Smythe's next call was to Dominick Martone, whose secretary told him that Martone was out of the office. Smythe left a message giving his cell phone number, but asked that Mr Martone not return the call after ten.

He pulled up in front of the Chinese restaurant and looked for Saison. He'd run fifteen minutes late because of an auto accident and he hoped that Saison hadn't decided to grab a taxi and leave. He was about to call the Frenchman's cell phone when he saw him exit the restaurant. Smythe blew the horn, and Saison lumbered in his direction, opened the passenger door, and piled into the seat, his body odor preceding him.

'What were you doing in there?' Smythe asked as he pulled away from the parking lot.

'What do you think I do in a Chinese restaurant, Smythe? It was a long walk. Two beers. Nothing else to drink in a Chinese restaurant, huh? They make lousy drinks, and Chinese wine is *une douche*. Everybody knows that. Where are we going?'

'Someplace quiet we can talk.'

Fifteen minutes later, and after Saison had worked on the contents of a pint bottle of wine he carried, they came to a stop sign in front of a building with the sign 'Bubs: A Gentleman's Club'.

110

'Hey, Smythe, we go in there, huh?'

'No.'

'What's the matter with you? The bitch, she's with her sister. I need a pretty woman, some inspiration, huh?'

'No,' Smythe said, and stepped on the gas.

Saison grabbed his arm. 'This is the place I want to go, Smythe. We go here or you take me home.'

Smythe was in no mood to argue. Besides, maybe this was a good place to have their conversation, somewhere dark and quiet. He sighed and turned into a parking space.

As they entered the club through soiled red velvet drapes, Smythe was assaulted by dizzying red-and-blue strobe lights and rock-'n-roll music cranked up to ear-splitting level. He blinked repeatedly as he tried to acclimate to the audio and visual chaos.

Two topless buxom young women, one white and one black, danced on a small stage, twirling about vertical poles and assuming classic sexy poses.

'Let's go,' Smythe told Saison.

The Frenchman ignored him and headed to seats at the edge of the stage, directly in front of the dancers. Smythe didn't move.

'You coming in or what?' a big man in a suit said.

'What? Oh, yes, I'm coming in but we're not staying.'

Smythe made his way to where Saison sat

111

ogling the dancers, and took a vacant seat next to him. 'Why did you pick this place?' he asked.

'You don't like it? What's wrong with it? The girls, they are *madone*, huh?'

'What? I can't hear you.'

Saison leaned closer and yelled, 'The girls, they are beautiful, *oui*?'

'We have to talk, Paul. Let's get out of here.'

Saison ignored him and waved over a waitress. 'Beer, Smythe? Wine?'

'No, nothing.'

'Come on, Smythe, we celebrate, huh? Pretty soon we be rich, huh?' He slapped Smythe on the back and said to the scantily-clad waitress, 'Two Kronenbourgs, OK?'

'I don't want a beer,' Smythe said.

One of the dancers came close, squatted down in front of Smythe, blew him a kiss and undulated her large bare brown breasts inches from his nose.

Saison laughed. 'Hey, she likes you, Smythe. Give her a tip.'

'What?' Smythe said, pulling back from her.

'Like this.' Saison pulled a Canadian dollar banknote from his shirt pocket, leaned toward the girl, and slipped the bill into the top of her G-string. 'Come on, Smythe, she dances for you.'

The combination of the loud music,

flashing lights, the whoops and hollers of drunken men, and the heavy odor of cheap perfume made Smythe dizzy.

'You know what you need, Smythe?' Saison shouted in his ear. 'You need a mistress, huh? Us French, we know how to live.'

Smythe thought of the naked Gina and a wave of nausea came and went. She was more beautiful than the girls performing in front of him, and she had class. She proudly showed off her gorgeous naked body only for the man she loved – him – *me*, he thought. Dancing near-naked for money disgusted him and he averted his eyes from the stage.

Their beers were delivered. Saison poked Smythe with his elbow. 'Pay the pretty lady,' he said.

'What? Oh, yes. How much?'

'Thirty,' the waitress said.

'Thirty? *Dollars?*'

She glared at him.

'All right,' he said as he pulled out his wallet, fished bills from it, and handed them to her. She counted the money and intensified her glare, a hand on her hip.

'Hey, Smythe, a tip for the *jolie fille.*'

'I already paid her thirty dollars,' Smythe protested loudly.

'This is all?' the waitress said, looking at the bills in her hand.—

'I already paid you plenty,' Smythe said.

'Smythe,' Saison said. 'Don't be cheap, huh? She's a working girl.'

'She can take her tip out of the thirty dollars I just gave her.'

A man sitting to Smythe's left wearing a red and yellow checkered flannel shirt and a Toronto Blue Jay baseball cap on backwards, said, 'Hey, what'd you do, stiff her?'

'I already paid for the beer and—'

Another man seated at the stage apron asked his friend, 'What'd he do?'

'He stiffed Monique.'

'What?' He leaned across his friend and snarled at Smythe, his words slurred, 'What are you, a troublemaker?'

'No, I—'

Smythe was gripped by the sudden tension, and decided to beat a hasty retreat. He didn't need to become involved in a fracas in such a dive; the thought of the police being called knotted his stomach. 'Let's go,' he told Saison.

Smythe stood, but the Toronto baseball fan clasped a large hand on his shoulder and pushed him back into his seat.

'Get your hand off me,' Smythe said.

Saison got between Smythe and the man in the baseball hat and said to him, *Imbécile! Ours puant!*

'What'd you call me?' the baseball fan said as he got to his feet.

'Please, Paul, let's go,' Smythe implored.

Saison was shoved in the chest. 'What'd you call me, you fucking Frog?'

Saison shoved back. Now he was confronted by the two customers.

Smythe grabbed Saison by the sleeve and yanked, but the big Frenchman didn't budge.

'Son-a-bitch didn't tip Monique.'

'Excuse my friend,' Smythe said, flashing a smile and trying to sound like the voice of reason, a diplomat. 'He's had a little too much to drink and—'

The large man in a suit who'd greeted Smythe as he entered the club suddenly appeared. 'You have a problem?' he asked Smythe.

'What? I can't hear with this music.'

'The young lady did something wrong?' the man asked.

'What?'

The manager turned to Saison. 'Get out 'a here,' he bellowed. 'You stink to high heaven.'

'He didn't tip me,' the waitress said.

'That's right,' Saison said. 'My friend forgot to give her a tip, huh?' He said to Smythe, 'She wants her tip.'

'But I already paid her thirty dollars,' Smythe said. 'For two beers.'

'The young lady works for tips,' the man said.

'That may be true, but thirty dollars for

two beers? That's outrageous.'

A second man in a suit approached. 'Problem?' he asked.

The first man said, 'He's complaining about the price for the beers and won't tip Monique.'

'Just a mistake,' Smythe said, a sheepish grin on his face. 'Everything is fine, just fine.' He elbowed Saison in the ribs. 'Let's go.'

The appearance of the two burly men cut into Saison's bravado. 'Some money for her, Smythe,' Saison said into his ear. 'Give her some money.'

Smythe handed Monique a five dollar bill, which seemed to satisfy her and her bosses. They stepped aside and allowed Smythe and Saison to leave.

Smythe said as they walked to his car, 'I've never seen anything like that. What a way to run a business. Why do you come to a filthy rattrap like this, Paul?'

'The girls, Smythe, the girls. Hey, what are you now, some sort of sissy boy, huh?'

'Disgusting,' Smythe said. 'Absolutely disgusting.'

'What is?'

'That ... that place.'

Saison shrugged, leaned against the car, took a swig from his pint bottle and lit a cigarette. 'So, why do you want to see me tonight?'

'I'll drive you home and tell you when we're there. You're sure Angelique won't be there?'

'No, she stays with her sister overnight. Two witches. OK, we go home and you tell me what's on your mind, huh?'

They sat at Saison's kitchen table. Saison poured himself a glass of wine, Smythe declined the offer. He said slowly, in a low tone, 'It's time, Paul.'

'What's time?'

'To put our plan into action.'

Smythe pulled an envelope from his inside jacket pocket and handed it to the Frenchman. Saison opened it and his eyes widened. *'Qu'est-ce que c'est?'*

'Five thousand dollars, Paul. A down payment.'

'Is all?'

Smythe kept his annoyance in check. 'Two weeks from this Friday night, August twenty-two, at nine forty-five,' he said. 'That's when you pull the switch, not a second before or a second after. We'll meet again next week to finalize the plan. Do you understand?'

'Yes, of course I understand. What do you think I am, some *Borné?* Some moron?'

'Of course not, Paul. It's just that ... well, it's just that this is the most important thing you or I will ever do in our lives. It can't fail. Everything must be done perfectly, no mistakes, no slip-ups. I'm depending on you, Paul. I have faith in you.'

Saison grinned at the compliment. 'Hey, Smythe, you can count on me. You know that, huh?'

'Yes, I know that, Paul. You have to be sure that you're scheduled to work that night, change your schedule if necessary. I also suggest that you not drink.'

Saison adopted an exaggerated look of hurt. 'Why you have to tell me that, Smythe? What do you think, that I drink too much?'

'No, not at all, Paul, but you'll have to be thinking extremely clearly that night. Just that night, Paul. Once you've shut down the plant you can leave Toronto, go to Montreal or Paris, go anywhere in the world you want to, drink and make love to pretty women, enjoy your life. But on Friday night, the twenty-second, you must be sober. Understand?'

'OK, OK, Smythe.'

'Good.' Smythe pulled a slip of paper from his shirt pocket, wrote on it, 'Friday, August twenty-two, nine forty-five pm,' and handed it to Saison. 'Just a reminder,' he said.

The hulking Frenchman tucked the paper in his shirt pocket, refilled his glass, and started to pour into the empty glass in front of Smythe. 'Come on, Smythe, drink up. We celebrate.'

Smythe stood and said, 'No, I have to be

going.' As he headed for the door his cell phone rang.

'Smythe? It's Dom Martone. You called?'

'Oh, yes. Thanks for getting back to me. I, ah, I really can't talk now.'

'That's OK, pal. I want you to come to the restaurant.'

'The one we met in before?'

'That's the one, pal. A half hour. Can you make it?'

'Yes, I'll be there.'

Saison laughed after Smythe had ended the call. 'A lady calls you, huh?'

'Ah, yes, Paul, a lady. I'll be in touch again soon.'

THIRTEEN

Smythe arrived at Martone's restaurant at a little before nine. The pizza parlor in front was virtually empty; only two tables were occupied. As Smythe came through the doors the faint sound of a tenor voice singing an aria from a familiar opera came through the brick back wall. Smythe tried to identify the opera but couldn't come up with the name. The pizza parlor manager approached. 'A table?' he asked.

'No. I'm here to see Mr Martone. He's expecting me.'

The manager went to the rear door and knocked. Hugo answered. The manager whispered something to him. Hugo squinted at Smythe to verify that he was a familiar face. He motioned, and Smythe entered the back room where the music was now louder. Hugo shut the door and retreated to the corner where his skinny partner sat.

Martone was seated at the table. A white napkin was tucked into his shirt collar, and he sang along with the recorded aria. Smythe took the second chair.

'You know this opera of course,' Martone said.

'Oh, sure, of course I do.'

'*Rigoletto*,' Martone said. 'Verdi. *La donna e mobile*.' He picked up where he had left off and accompanied the tenor in a voice that surprised Smythe. He sounded as good to him as anyone he'd heard sing at the musicales at the house. The aria ended and Martone laughed while surreptitiously dabbing at one eye.

'So, what's up?' Martone asked.

'I'm ready to move with our project.'

'Good, good, like to hear that.'

Smythe looked back at Hugo and his colleague before saying to Martone, 'Could we talk someplace more private?'

'These are my associates, Smythe. Don't worry about them.'

Smythe nodded. 'OK,' he said. 'The date is set.'

'Good. What is it?'

Smythe extended his hands palms-up, like Marlon Brando in *The Godfather*.

Martone grinned. 'Yeah, yeah,' he said, 'You want the money.' He abruptly stood and waved his two bodyguards from the room.

'OK,' he said. 'Now we get down to brass tacks as they say. You have the date the lights go out. I have the million bucks for that information.'

Smythe corrected, 'A million, two hundred fifty thousand.'

Martone laughed. 'Yeah, yeah, I wasn't shorting you, Smythe. A million two fifty *less* the fifty Gs I gave you.'

'Of course. I haven't forgotten that. Do you have the money with you?'

Another laugh from the Mafia boss. 'Oh, sure, Smythe. It's in my pocket. You know what I think?'

'What?'

'I think that you may be some sort 'a genius, setting up this blackout and all, but you're also dumb as hell.'

Smythe said nothing.

'You know how big a bundle a million bucks makes? I'd say it's around four cubic feet.' He gestured with his hands to indicate how high and wide that was. 'It maybe weighs twenty, twenty-five pounds. You think I walk around with a fucking wheelbarrow filled with hundred dollar bills?'

'No, Dom, I—'

'But forget about me walking down the street with a wheelbarrow. What about *you*, Smythe? What the hell are you goin' to do with a pile like that? What do you think, pal, that I'll give you an envelope full 'a ten thousand dollar bills? Ha! You know the biggest bill we got here in Canada? A hundred. Used to be there were bigger bills but no more. Hundreds. That's the biggest bills we got. So how many of those bills do you figure you'll be hauling around? Do the math, Smythe. Ten thousand hundred-dollar bills. Four cubic feet of greenbacks, twenty, twenty-five pounds. So tell me, Smythe, what the fuck are you goin' to do with that? Take it to some bank? Forget about it. Anything over ten Gs they report it to the feds. You gotta launder it, Smythe. Not that it's my business. Hell, I give you money and you're on your own. What the fuck do I care what you do with it? But I like you, Smythe. I just figured that I'd give you some free advice.'

'And I ... well, I appreciate that, Dom.'

'I got another question. You intend to hang around Toronto once this thing goes down?'

'No, I—'

'But you got a wife, a nice lady, loves opera, does a good job with the COC. She know what you're doing?'

'Oh, no, of course not. The truth is that once I have the money I plan to leave, go someplace far away. You see, Dom, our marriage isn't a happy one. Cynthia is a—'

'You've got problems with her?'

'Yes, I suppose that you could say that.'

'She'll make trouble for you once you split?'

'Oh, yes, I mean she will ... make trouble for me. But I'll be far away and—'

Martone reached across the table and

placed his hand on Smythe's arm. 'I gotta admit something to you, Smythe. At first I had my ... well, what you'd call my reservations. I mean, you come off like a nice guy and all but I thought you might be a little ... a little whack-a-ding-hoy.'

'Pardon?'

'Nuts. It's a Chinaman's expression. Not all there. Anyway, I've got a different view of you now. I like you, Smythe, almost like you were family.'

'That's really nice, Dom. Thank you.'

'And because I like you like family I can take care of your wife if you want.'

'Take care of her?'

Martone winked. 'Look, pal, sometimes things have to be done because things have to be done. *Capisce?*'

'Are you suggesting that—?'

Martone raised his hand as though to signal that Smythe should stop talking. 'All I'm saying is that since you won't be hanging around to let your family enjoy the money – and you know how much I believe in family – that your wife might be in a position to make it tough on you, maybe even testify against you. That wouldn't be good for you Smythe – or for me.'

'I can't believe I'm hearing this.'

'Get off your high horse, Smythe. Just think about what I said. I know some people who take care of this sort 'a thing, and it don't cost much, ten, fifteen Gs tops.'

Smythe worked hard to calm his frazzled nerves. When he felt that he had, he said, 'I was going to ask you, Dom, to make sure that no one is ever hurt in our joint endeavor, no one *physically* hurt that is. If I thought that that was even a possibility I—'

Martone stared at Smythe.

'No offense,' Smythe quickly added, 'but it is important to me that the only damage done is monetary.'

Martone's face softened into what passed for an understanding grin, which calmed Smythe. The Mafia chieftain stood, came around the table, and placed his hands on Smythe's bony shoulders. His fingers dug into them, and Smythe winced against the pain. Martone leaned over and said into his ear, 'You got to stop worrying, Smythe. Tell you what. You tell me where to deliver the money tomorrow. I deliver it and you give me the time and date. How's that sound?'

'That sounds fine, Dom.'

Martone released his grip and went to the door. 'Where do you want the loot delivered?'

Smythe gave him the address of his rented office.

'Two o'clock,' Martone said. 'I won't personally be there. My associates will deliver it. Anybody asks, you say it's books in the package. When my associates deliver the money, you give them a sealed envelope that has the date and time inside. We understand each other?'

'Oh, yes, we do,' Smythe said, standing. 'It sounds like a good plan.'

'One other thing. I already started contacting business associates of mine about buying in. One of them – he's a big man in Philadelphia – wants to personally meet my partner. Same with a business associate in Baltimore. I told them no problem. We can do it in one day, day after tomorrow.' He laughed. 'This time it's me who gives the time and place. Keep the date open. I'll be in touch. Oh, by the way, pal, COC is having another fundraiser tomorrow night. Maybe you'd like to drop by and donate a few grand. Be sure to get a receipt. It's tax-deductable.'

Smythe stopped by his rented office on the way home. Gina had sent an email in which she gave him the name and contact information of her 'banker friend'. She assured Smythe that her friend had many contacts, and could be trusted to deposit any monies sent to him for their joint account. Smythe emailed back, thanked her, and signed off with a string of endearing phrases.

As he got in the car and headed home he thought about his meeting with Martone. The Mafioso's suggestion that Cynthia be hurt in some way was worse than unsettling, but he was confident that he'd made his point about no one being physically injured. He then thought about tomorrow when a million dollars plus would be delivered to him. That thought spawned giggles, and he had to fight to maintain control of the car.

Dominick Martone was also giddy as he sat in the rear seat of the Town Car driven by Hugo and his second 'associate'. He'd already more than covered his investment with Smythe through pledges from compatriots in Buffalo, Boston, and Detroit. In fact, he was already into a profit – almost two million above what he would pay Smythe. And with many more cities to pitch, including Baltimore and Philadelphia where he would travel with Smythe in two days, that profit would grow.

Of course, it all depended upon Smythe coming through with the blackout as promised.

If he didn't....

FOURTEEN

Clarence Miller III sat in his white panel truck with 'Miller – Electrical Contractor' written in large red letters on the sides. He had two such trucks to use when on a case. The other was painted black and its white sign read 'Miller – The Happy Exterminator.' A nondescript black sedan was parked next to the truck. An employee at Miller Discreet Investigations had left it there to give Clarence a choice of vehicles to use should he choose to continue following his subject, Carlton Smythe.

Clarence had inherited the private investigation agency six years ago from his father, who'd died with his boots on so to speak. The elder Miller had been wearing the sort of chest waders used by trout fishermen while conducting surveillance on a contractor suspected of polluting a river. He'd suffered a mild heart attack, which wouldn't have been fatal had he been able to seek medical assistance. But the sudden pain in his chest and left arm caused him to lose his footing and to fall into the stream. The waders soon filled up and, as the death certificate read, he'd died of drowning.

Clarence's older brother had wanted nothing to do with the agency – he considered himself a poet and novelist and had fled to Hawaii – leaving the agency, which was quite successful, to the younger Clarence.

He was parked in the parking lot in front of the building in which Carlton Smythe had rented a temporary office. It was one in the afternoon. He'd seen Smythe enter the building a few minutes earlier. Now, he would wait until his subject reappeared and would follow him to wherever he went next. He didn't mind the long waits while conducting surveillance. Other private detectives he knew hated that aspect of the job, but Clarence considered long stakeouts to be time for reflection, to keep up with his reports, and to play Angry Birds on his iPad.

On this day he wrote in the log he'd started when taking on the Smythe case. He'd promised Mrs Carlton Smythe and her mother that his reports to them would be detailed and frequent, and Clarence Miller always kept his word.

He'd commenced shadowing Smythe late afternoon on the previous day. His notes from that day, with times and dates accurately recorded, as well as weather conditions, read:

Entered office rental building at 2:27pm (obviously rents space there, will check) – exited building at 5:11pm – got in car. I followed. Subject drove to shopping center near Power-Con electric utility – parked in front of Panda Gardens, Chinese restaurant – waited 15 minutes before a large man with greasy hair and beard stubble came from restaurant and got in subject's car. Subject drove for 15 minutes before turning into parking lot in front of a strip club, Bubs. Subject and unidentified male (check identity) entered club, came from club 29 minutes later – took telephoto of both men while standing outside subject's car – seemed upset – left parking lot and went to a rundown 3-story apartment building in French section – went inside – checked names in lobby. Observed them through window on 3rd floor – only name with apartment on 3rd floor is Paul Saison – subject exited at 8:20pm – drove to Martone's pizza restaurant on St Clair in Italian section – exited 24 minutes later – drove to office rental building – was inside 17 minutes. Subject left and drove home – weather partly cloudy with occasional breaks of sun.

At a few minutes before two o'clock a black Town Car pulled into a space three removed

130

from Clarence's panel truck. He watched out of the corner of his eye as a big man with a shaved head, and a smaller slender man with a prominent nose got out, opened the trunk, and the big man removed an obviously heavy cardboard box wrapped in tape.

Hugo and his Mafia colleague carried the box into the lobby where Smythe waited.

'This is for Mr Smith,' Hugo told the receptionist. 'Books.'

'It's Smythe,' Carlton said as he came to the desk. 'Like in *Blithe Spirit*.'

Hugo gave him an angry look.

'Oh, this is for you,' Smythe said, handing Hugo the envelope in which he'd written the date and time of the blackout.

Smythe carried the box back to his office, shut and locked the door, and used scissors to cut away the tape. His heart pounded and he began to sweat as he pulled back the box's flaps and peered inside. Beneath a layer of newspaper was the money, neatly bound packages of hundred dollar bills.

Smythe wondered whether he was about to have a coronary. He gasped for air, and placed his hands over his face. When the initial shock had subsided, he closed the box and shoved it beneath the desk, covering it with file folders. His pipe dream, his what-if? had worked. No, he realized, it was *working*, but he still had a long way to go to bring it to a happy conclusion.

His conversation with Martone the previous night had been sobering. Although he'd known from the outset that getting the money to Argentina would be a challenge, and a big one at that, he'd pushed aside that concern – until now.

What do I do with a million, two hundred thousand dollars in cash?

He spent the next hour formulating a plan. Obviously having all that cash sitting in his rented office was a risk, but what choice did he have? He decided on a course of action, which included taking a portion of the money with him to his pool house office at the rear of his home. In addition, he would have to assume the risk of sending various amounts of it to Gina and her banker friend, using Federal Express and UPS. He went online and got the names of other international shipping companies, including DHL and NEX Worldwide Express. They wouldn't question what was in the boxes he would use, would they? And if they did, he would say that the boxes contained books. There was no way that he could carry that much cash aboard an aircraft, although his previous experience with transporting thirty thousand dollars in his suitcase and on his person had gone smoothly. After much soul searching, and conjuring approaches, he resolved to do whatever he could and hope that it worked.

As Smythe formulated plans to get the money to Argentina, Clarence Miller continued his vigilance in the parking lot. He'd gotten a photograph of Hugo and his buddy as they came from the building, and had noted the car's plate number. He was in the process of making notes when a text message came through on his iPad. It was from a private investigator in Buenos Aires, Popi Domingo, with whom Miller had forged an alliance. Miller's deceased father had established relationships with other investigators around the globe, which his son made good use of. Because Cynthia Smythe had told Miller of her husband's frequent trips to Buenos Aires, he'd contacted his Argentinean cohort and asked him to be on tap should his client's husband make another trip there.

Consider it done, the message read.

Inside the building, Smythe dragged the box from beneath the desk, opened it, and began laying out packages of hundred dollar bills in neat piles, and placed small pink Post-its on which he'd written on each. One pile would come home with him and be hidden in the pool house. Other piles were designated for Federal Express, UPS, DHL, and NEX Worldwide Express. He carefully measured each pile to determine how large the boxes must be that he would pick up from the various shipping companies. The final pile would be kept in his rented office until it was time to leave the country. Cash in that pile would travel with him along with what he sequestered at home.

Satisfied, he returned the cash to the box and slid it beneath the desk, trusting that it would be safe for a few days.

He was unaware that he was being followed by Clarence Miller as he drove home. The investigator waited an hour outside the Smythe home until he was relieved by another investigator from the agency, a former Canadian Air Force officer named Janet Kudrow, who would remain there for the rest of the night in the event Smythe left the house.

But Smythe had no intention of leaving that evening. He and Cynthia had dinner together, and settled in after the meal to watch a movie on TV. He'd told her that he'd be gone the next day, a short business trip.

'Argentina again?' she'd said, not unpleasantly.

'No, ah, Philadelphia. Another potential client.'

'That's good,' she'd said.

'Be back tomorrow night,' he said.

'That's the sort of trip I like to see you take, Carlton, less stressful. Remember, you are not getting any younger.'

The film, *Topkapi*, a classic caper movie, came on the screen and Carlton and Cynthia Smythe spent the next two hours silently enjoying it.

No movie was playing in the apartment that Paul Saison shared with his live-in paramour, Angelique. She'd returned from her visit to her sister in Montreal exhausted after the three hundred mile drive, and in a combative mood. She expected Saison to be in his usual testy mood, but was surprised to be confronted by an upbeat, almost gregarious version of the large Frenchman. She immediately noted that he'd showered and shaved, and wore a fresh shirt and pants. He hugged her and said, 'I am so happy that you are home, *ma chérie*. Come sit, I make you a drink.'

'You're drunk,' she said.

He laughed. 'A little, but I am a happy drunk, huh?'

'You're always drunk,' she said.

He did what passed for a pirouette and said, 'Drunk with love *ma chérie*, drunk with good fortune.'

'What good fortune?' she asked as she sat at the kitchen table, skepticism on her pretty round face, and watched as he poured vodka into a tall water glass, added ice, and presented it to her.

He raised the glass he'd been drinking

from and said, 'Money, Angelique, *beaucoup* de money.'

'What did you do, you buffoon, rob a bank while I was away?'

He sat next to her and tickled beneath her chin with his index finger. 'Oh,' he said, 'you always think the bad things about me, always think that Saison doesn't know what he is doing, huh?'

'When did you *ever* know what you were doing?'

He adopted an exaggerated expression of hurt. 'You shoot arrows into my heart with that talk.' He leaned close and said, 'Maybe you think different about me when I have a quarter million dollars, and more when it is done.'

'When *what* is done?'

'Ah, ha, you would like to know, *oui?*' He sat back, a satisfied expression on his face. 'Well, I am no fool.'

Which was exactly what she considered him.

'I'm going to bed,' she said. 'You're a drunk *and* a crazy man.'

'No, no, stay. I will tell you, but not too much,' he said, grabbing her wrist. 'You call me a crazy man? Hah! You want to know who is a crazy man? I tell you. Smythe, he is a crazy man.'

'Smythe?'

'Smythe. He used to be my boss at the plant, remember?'

'Oh, him. What about him?'

He lowered his voice to a whisper. 'He has come up with a plan that will make me a rich man.'

'Plan? What plan?'

'What do you think, that I tell you the plan? Hah! You think I don't know what I'm doing? I tell you something, *ma chérie*. You treat me like dirt, huh, like some mangy dog? You will see that Paul Saison, he knows what he is doing.'

She guffawed. 'Paul Saison knows what he is doing? Paul Saison is a *crétin*.'

'Who tells you that? Your sister, the witch?'

'My sister knows what you are. Why do you think she always tells me to get away from you?'

'Ha! Where do you go, huh? Your sister, she is an ugly witch, no man for her.'

'It just so happens that she has a boyfriend, a wonderful boyfriend, and they plan to be married.'

'Poor bastard.'

The drink that Saison had just consumed tipped him over the edge from tipsy to drunk. He stood unsteadily, grabbed the edge of the table for support, and clamped his other hand on her breast, which she angrily pushed away.

'Hey, come on,' he said. 'We go make some love, huh?'

'In a pig's ass,' she said. 'Keep your paws

off me.'

Angelique stood and took a step toward the bedroom. 'You sleep out here,' she said.

'No, bitch, *you* sleep out here.'

'I'll be gone in the morning,' she said.

'Good. Go to your witch of a sister. I'll be better off.' With that he stumbled away, went into the bedroom, and slammed the door.

Angelique cried quietly. She knew that her threat to be gone the next morning was empty, unrealistic. But she would leave one day, of that she was certain. She'd discussed it with her sister, who urged her to get away and to come live with her in Montreal. She would wait until Saison was away for a few days before packing up her belongings, which weren't much, and escaping the smelly, hairy ape for good.

Buoyed by that conviction, she prepared to toss sheets on the couch and settle in. Before she got up from the table she noticed a scrap of paper under the pepper mill. She picked it up and read: ***Friday, August twenty-two, nine forty-five pm***. It meant nothing to her and she dropped it on the table. But as she scrunched up between the sheets and duvet, she thought of what Saison had said, that he would soon be rich. More drunken braggadocio? For some reason this was different from his usual rants. Why was he in touch again with his boss from a year and a half ago, Mr Smythe? He'd called Smythe a crazy man who had a plan. What could the plan be?

Her final thoughts before drifting off were of her sister and new boyfriend, which made her smile. She loved Celine, and was happy that she'd found the right man. Antoine Arnaud seemed like a nice guy. He wasn't handsome, but wasn't bad looking either. He was in his early forties and had never married, although Celine assured Angelique that he'd had plenty of opportunities. Celine appreciated that he was a solid citizen, a responsible fellow who worked as a special agent for the Canada Border Services Agency, the sort of man whom Angelique pledged she would seek once free of Saison. How she ever got involved with him in the first place was beyond her. But no matter. She'd soon be rid of him, and she giggled as she thought of his drunken claim that he was about to be rich.

Celine would get a kick out of that tall tale when they spoke on the phone the next day.

FIFTEEN

Martone had instructed Smythe to take the five thirty am ferry the following morning from the Eireann Quay to the Toronto Islands where the Billy Bishop Toronto City Airport was located. The airport, named after a Canadian World War I flying ace, was home to only a few small, regularly scheduled airlines but was a busy hub for corporate and private aircraft.

The islands were four hundred feet from the quay; it was the shortest ferry ride in North America. Smythe found a rare space in the small, crowded parking lot, unaware that Clarence Miller's investigator, Janet Kudrow, had followed him and gotten in line to purchase a ticket.

Smythe boarded the two hundred-passenger Marilyn Bell I ferry along with airport workers and early morning passengers, stood at the railing and wondered what the meeting Martone had arranged would be like. It was an overcast day; Smythe could feel rain in his bones – along with fear.

The meeting had been scheduled for

Smythe to meet other Mafioso from Baltimore and Philadelphia who were interested in buying the blackout information from Martone. What would they be like? What would they ask him? Would the nervousness he felt be obvious to them and possibly derail the project? He didn't have much time to ponder these things because before he knew it the ferry had docked and he'd joined the line of people and cars leaving it.

Martone had instructed him to come to a private aviation hangar located at the far end of the airport. Smythe spotted the building in the distance and walked slowly towards it. He hadn't anticipated having to attend such a meeting when he put his plan into play, and the tension he'd felt earlier now intensified. As he got closer to the hangar he saw Martone standing next to a sleek, white twin-engine jet aircraft without markings. Smythe recognized Hugo and his constant companion, but there were also two other men cut from the same mold. Martone waved to Smythe and motioned for him to pick up his pace.

'Hey, pal,' Martone said, 'I was getting worried. Come on, we got to get moving.'

They boarded the jet. Two pilots sat in the cockpit. One of them came back and pulled up the short stairs and secured the door. 'All set?' he asked.

'Let's go,' said Martone.

Smythe sat across a pull-down table from Martone; his 'associates' took seats behind them.

'Is this your plane?' Smythe asked, not sure whether he should.

'Mine to use,' was Martone's reply. 'You got the delivery yesterday?'

'Yes, thank you.'

'It was all there?'

'I didn't bother counting it. I'm sure that—'

'I like to hear that. Trust is everything in a business deal. You don't have trust, you got nothing. Am I right?'

'Oh, yes, you're absolutely right, Dom. We're going to Philadelphia?'

'Yeah, sort of. Outside Philly. I got my Baltimore associates to come up, save us making two stops. We'll be back in Toronto in time for the COC fundraiser tonight.'

'That's good,' Smythe said, having forgotten about it.

Kudrow had stood many yards away and watched the take-off. She called Miller, who told her to go home. He would check later with the private aviation company about where the plane was headed. 'I have to meet with the client this morning,' he said. 'Good job, Janet. Get some rest.'

Once at cruising altitude, one of the pilots came into the passenger cabin and broke out Danish pastries, coffee, and juice.

'Fancy, huh?' Martone said as he bit into a cherry Danish. 'Go on, pal, eat up.'

Smythe did as instructed and silently peered through the window at the thick, gray cloud cover below, casting occasional nervous glances at Hugo and his colleagues.

Martone browsed the latest issue of *Opera Magazine*. 'Hey, catch this,' he said at one point, 'the Chinese are goin' nuts over Wagner.' He correctly pronounced Wagner with a V.

'Interesting,' Smythe said.

'I keep thinking I ought to do some business in China,' Martone said, 'expand my horizons. One thing for certain, those Chinese sure have the dough.'

After breakfast had been cleared, Smythe said, 'Dom, about this meeting we're going to: what do your business associates want to know from me?'

Martone slapped him on the arm. 'Relax, pal. They just want to see that there really is this guy named Smythe who says he's gonna make everything go black on the twenty-second.' He paused and adopted a serious tone. 'Everything's going OK, am I right? No hitches?'

'No, no. Everything is set, Dom. No hitches.'

'Good. Settle back, pal, grab a nap. We'll be there before you know it.'

I wish we'd never get there, Smythe thought.

Cynthia had pretended to be asleep when Smythe left before sun-up. She waited until eight to call Miller to say that her husband was gone and that it would be a good time to come to the house.

When he arrived at nine, Cynthia and her mother were waiting. They sat in the kitchen and Miller pulled photos and notes from his briefcase.

'Is he with another woman?' Cynthia immediately asked.

'No, not yet,' Miller replied, 'but it's still early in the investigation. Does he have plans for another trip to Argentina?'

'None that he's told me about.'

'If he does, let me know right away. My man in Buenos Aires is ready to check his activities once he's there. Now, let me show you some photos.'

The first one he laid on the table was of Smythe and Saison in the parking lot of the strip club, Bubs.

'Disgusting,' Mrs Wiggins said, 'patronizing a place like that.'

'He and this other man weren't in there very long,' Miller reported. 'You know who he is?' He handed Cynthia a magnifying glass through which she examined Saison's face.

'No, he's not familiar to me,' she said.

'I think I've got his name,' said Miller.

'Saison.'

'Saison? Saison?' Cynthia muttered. 'Carlton used to talk about someone named Saison who worked for him at Power-Can. He didn't like him, said he was a gambler and a drunk.'

'I have people checking into his background,' Miller said as he laid the second photo on top of the first. It was of Hugo and his fellow Mafioso coming out of the building where Smythe rented temporary quarters.

'I recognize them,' said Cynthia. 'They work for Dominick Martone.'

'The Mafia chief?'

'I hesitate calling him that,' Cynthia said. 'Why did you take *their* picture?' she asked.

'They carried a big box into the building where your husband rents an office.'

'Rents an office? Carlton?'

'Seems like it, Mrs Smythe. They went in carrying the box but came out without it.'

He placed the next picture on the pile, this of Smythe exiting Martone's restaurant. 'Seems like he and Mr Martone are pretty friendly,' the investigator said.

'Carlton said he'd been talking to him about a possible business deal,' Cynthia said.

'I'll be finding out more,' Miller said. 'One of my other investigators followed your husband this morning when he left the house.'

'He said he was going to Philadelphia to see a potential client.'

'He went to the Billy Bishop airport on Toronto Islands, took off with some men in a private jet.'

'What men?'

'My colleague didn't recognize any of them. She didn't have a chance to grab a photo without being observed. I'll swing by the airport when I leave here and see what I can come up with.'

'Is there anything else?' Mrs Wiggins asked.

'Not at the moment, ma'am, but we'll stay on it.'

Cynthia smiled. 'I'm relieved,' she said.

'Why?' her mother asked.

'I don't know what Carlton is up to these days – it must have to do with business – but at least there isn't another woman.'

'How can you say that?' his mother said. 'He's obviously depraved, perverted, visiting one of those sewers called stripper clubs. Disgusting!'

'Yes, ma'am,' Miller said. 'Remember to let me know if he plans another trip to Buenos Aires. I'll be back in touch.'

The jet descended through the dense cloud cover and into clear air. Smythe looked out his window in search of an airport and a city, but saw only verdant rolling hills. The pilot turned sharply to the left, snapped the aircraft back into straight-and-level flight, and proceeded to do what Smythe could only describe as a dive. He clenched his teeth, fiercely gripped his armrests, and his stomach tightened as the ground rapidly came up outside his window. Moments later the plane slammed down on the runway, bounced up, then settled as the pilot reversed his engines' thrust and applied the brakes.

Smythe saw nothing but green hills until the plane turned off the runway and taxied. Now what looked like a castle, an imposing two-story stone building with turrets on either end, came into view.

'Where are we?' he asked Martone.

'The place where we're meeting my business associates.'

Smythe watched through the window as the plane came to a stop a hundred yards from the building. The door opened and two men stood on the long stone porch that ran the width of the house. The jet's engines shut down and the co-pilot came from the cockpit to lower the stairs. Hugo and another Mafioso left the plane, followed by Smythe, then Martone, with the remaining two bodyguards bringing up the rear. As Smythe stood at the foot of the stairs, other men exited the house and joined the original two.

'Good to see you, Tony,' Martone said, shaking hands with one of the men on the porch, a tall, angular man with a swarthy complexion and a long, sad face that reminded Smythe of a bloodhound.

'Same here, Dom. You have a nice flight?'

'Oh, yeah, smooth as silk. Tony, this is the guy I told you about, Mr Smythe.'

Smythe shook Tony's outstretched hand. As he did, Tony's black eyes bored holes in him, and he averted his gaze and looked back to where the plane had landed, a long strip of black asphalt nestled in the surrounding hills.

'What say we get this meeting underway?' Martone said. 'Alphonse here?'

'On his way,' replied Tony. 'Come on inside. We've got a nice spread laid out.'

They were led to a dining room – Smythe thought of medieval banquet rooms from the movies in which dozens of men in robes decided someone's fate – where a side table contained an array of cold cuts, breads, crab claws, and other dishes. Two young women wearing black turtleneck shirts and white aprons stood behind the food. A much larger table in the center of the room had places set for four.

Smythe nibbled on a few items, but the last thing on his mind was eating. He'd never been in such circumstances before, and had to struggle to keep his anxiety in check. No one engaged him in conversation. Martone and the man named Tony huddled in a corner, plates of food in their hands, while the other men gravitated to the perimeter of the huge room. Smythe sidled up to Hugo. 'This is some fancy place,' he said.

Hugo hunched his large shoulders and said, 'Yeah.'

'You come here often?' Smythe asked.

'No.'

Smythe forced a laugh. 'That's what men say when they're trying to pick up a woman in a bar,' he said. 'You come here often?'

Hugo stared, and Smythe walked away to an unoccupied corner. He'd no sooner reached it when Hugo and four others quickly left the room, returning a few minutes later with another entourage led by a short, roly-poly man whose black hair was pasted to his head, and who was followed by four other 'Hugos'.

'Hey, Alphonse,' Martone said, going to him and shaking his hand. 'Glad you could make it. You drive here from Baltimore?'

'Yeah, we drive here, Dom. I see you fly here in your private airplane. Business must be good in Canada.'

'I rent it. I got shares in it.'

'Me, I don't like to fly,' Tony said. 'I don't trust those fuckin' airplanes and pilots.'

'Hey, whatever works for you,' Alphonse said.

'What do you say we get started?' Martone interjected. 'We sit down and work this thing out.' As though suddenly realizing that Smythe was present and that he was the reason for them being there, he waved the Canadian over.

'You already met Tony,' Martone said to Smythe. 'Say hello to Alphonse, from Baltimore. Tony's from Philly. This place we're in, it's Tony's. What do you call it, Tony, your castle?'

'That's right. Looks like a fuckin' castle, don't it?'

'You should wear one 'a those metal suits, like the knights wore.'

'Maybe I will,' Tony said.

'Sit down, sit down,' Martone said. 'Let's get this little confab underway.' He motioned for the waitresses to leave the room, which they did, escorted by two of Martone's men.

Martone sat at the head of the table, and directed Smythe to sit to his left. Alphonse took a chair next to Smythe; Tony sat across from him.

'I called this sit-down because you, Tony, and you, Alphonse, wouldn't come in on a deal with me until you met my partner, Smythe here. Now I'll be honest with you, I felt disrespected, but I told myself to not let that get in the way of a good deal. Maybe what bothered me was that my generosity was being questioned. Hell, I didn't have to bring you, Tony, or you, Alphonse, into this business arrangement. Other bosses didn't disrespect me when I offered them in on the deal. They thanked me for being generous, for sharing the wealth with them, no questions asked, just faith in me as a man of my word, a man of honor. Don't get me wrong. I'm not somebody who holds a grudge. You all know that. So I agreed to bring my partner with me for this sit-down so you could ask him questions.'

'You say you got Carmine in Boston to come in on the deal, Dom?' Alphonse asked.

'That's right, no questions asked. He came in on my word, the way it should be.'

'No offense, Dom,' said Tony, 'but I don't put up the kind of money you're asking without some info. Just good business.'

'What about New York?' Alphonse asked.

'I meet with Vinnie tomorrow. He's coming to Toronto.'

As the conversation continued between the mob leaders, Smythe squirmed in his chair and tried to look disinterested. He'd seen all the Mafia movies – the three *Godfather* films, *Goodfellas*, *A Bronx Tale*, *Casino*, *Donnie Brasco* – and was always fascinated with the 'sit-down' scenes in which the heads of crime families met to carve out territories and to resolve family differences.

But this wasn't a movie, and he wished it was. Most of all he wished he wasn't there, and envisioned himself in Buenos Aires in Gina's arms.

'OK,' Tony said, turning from Martone and facing Smythe, 'so you're the guy who's supposed to make this work, make the lights go out.'

'Yes, sir, I—'

'I don't understand,' Tony continued. 'How do you pull this off, make the lights go out?'

'I'd rather not—'

'With all due respect,' Martone said, 'I think your question is out of order.'

'Out of *what* order?' Tony said.

'You're asking him to reveal how he does it,' Martone said. 'If you knew how he did it you wouldn't need him – or me.'

Alphonse laughed. 'Maybe that's what Tony's getting at,' he said. 'Cut out the middleman.'

With Martone backing him, Smythe sat up straighter and said, 'I didn't think in coming here that I'd be asked to reveal my secrets. All I can say is that I can see to it that all electrical power along the eastern seaboard will be cut off at a precise time on a specific date. What you decide to do with that knowledge is your business. It's of no concern to me, any more than how I do it should concern you.'

He checked their faces for reactions to his statement. Alphonse looked at Tony, who looked at Martone, and all three looked at Smythe.

'He speaks the truth,' Martone said.

'So OK, you can pull this off,' said Tony, 'but how do we know that you will? I mean, what if you and Dominick pocket our money and then you decide to split?'

'I have no intention of splitting,' Smythe said, 'until the lights have gone out. As for a guarantee, you'll have to take my word for it.'

'The way others have,' Martone said. 'And I will say this: you know me as a successful businessman, not a fool. Mr Smythe answers to me, Dominick Martone, which should be good enough for everyone at this table.'

The next fifteen minutes were spent with the three mob leaders arguing about honor and trust. At one point when Alphonse said something to Martone that contained a veiled threat, Hugo and another Martone henchman stood and came up behind Alphonse, which prompted two of Alphonse's men to do the same with Martone.

Martone slapped his hand on the table and snapped, 'Enough! We sound like schoolboys, not the grown businessmen that we are. I say this meeting is adjourned. You want in on the deal or you don't. I don't need you, but when it's over and others have made their millions, do not come to Dominick Martone and say that he wasn't generous and didn't give you an opportunity to share in the spoils.'

Alphonse held up his hand and said, 'Dominick is right. I am in, under the terms I discussed with him before.'

All eyes went to Tony. He shrugged, made a gesture of acquiescence, and said, 'Count me in.'

The three men stood and shook hands. The meeting was over, and Smythe drew a prolonged sigh of relief.

They left the stone mansion and gathered at the plane where the pilot sat in the cockpit, and the co-pilot stood at the top of the short flight of stairs waiting for the passengers to board. There were hugs between the three mob bosses.

'It was a real pleasure meeting you, gentlemen,' Smythe said to Alphonse and Tony.

'Same here,' Alphonse said. 'Just remember that if things don't go the way they're supposed to go we'll see you again.'

His meaning was crystal clear.

As Smythe was about to go up the stairs he looked beyond the other men and saw two cars kicking up dust as they roared toward them.

'We got trouble,' Tony said

Smythe stood alone as everyone broke

away and headed for the house, although some men crouched behind statuary of nymphs and lions and drew their weapons. The cars came to a swerving stop, their occupants emerging with guns blazing and using the vehicles to shield them from return fire. A flurry of bullets kicked up grass at Smythe's feet. He ran to the left, then to the right, his only thought at that moment of the movie, *The In-Laws*, in which Peter Falk yelled at Alan Arkin, 'Serpentine, Serpentine', as they ran figure-of-eights while being attacked by Central American bandits.

Martone, who'd boarded the plane with Hugo and the others, screamed at Smythe to join him.

Smythe stumbled as he made for the plane, righted himself, and scrambled up the stairs. The co-pilot closed the door and rejoined the pilot up front. The engines were started and the cockpit crew started going over its pre-flight checklist when Martone yelled at the pilot through the open cockpit door, 'Let's go, let's go! Get this fucking plane outta here.'

'What's going on?' Smythe asked Martone, who held a handgun. Hugo and the others had also drawn their weapons. 'Is there trouble?' As soon as he said it, he realized the stupidity of the question.

'Move it, move it!' Martone shouted at the

pilots.

Outside the plane, fire from Alphonse, Tony, and their crime family members kept their attackers pinned behind their cars as the pilot gunned the engines and the jet started to move. He spun it around and headed for the landing strip, the jet engine noise accompanied by the sound of rapid-fire gunshots. Two shots punctured the plane's fuselage, one of them reaching the cabin and knocking a glass off a table. Smythe slid off his seat and lay on the floor, his hands over his head. A minute later, after a fast, bumpy taxi to the strip, the engines were advanced to maximum power and the plane careened down the makeshift runway until its wheels lifted off and they were air-borne.

'Son-of-a-bitch,' Martone growled. 'Can you believe that?'

Smythe pulled himself to a sitting position and said, 'Who were those men in the cars? The police?'

Martone looked at him as though he'd committed an offensive bodily act. 'Police my ass. That's a rival gang from Philly. Tony's been in a war with them for months. You OK?'

'Me?' Smythe said, returning to his seat and brushing off his suit. 'Yes, I'm all right, Dom. It's just that I've never been involved in anything like this.'

'Hey, pal, relax. Happens now and then in business.'

'Will Tony and Alphonse be OK?'

A shrug from Martone. 'Maybe, maybe not. Not my problem.' He called out to the cockpit crew, 'How about some food back here?'

Later that night, after returning home from the COC fundraiser which Martone hadn't attended, much to Smythe's relief, he sat with Cynthia watching the ten o'clock news on TV.

'Was it a successful trip today?' she asked.

'Yeah, I think so.'

The news anchor reported, 'In news from the States, a gang war between rival crime families in the Philadelphia area broke out today when one of the gangs attacked another at a mansion owned by one of the families. Police were called but arrived after the attack had ended. Two lower-level men belonging to the crime family allegedly headed by Anthony "Hounddog" Russo were shot dead. According to police, a war between rival gangs has been brewing for several months. No one has been arrested and charged with the shooting.'

'How anyone could associate with such people is beyond me,' Cynthia said. 'It's like men who frequent striptease clubs.'

She glanced at Carlton, whose attention

was fixed on the screen as though he hadn't heard what she'd said, which was just as well.

'Carlton, do you think Dominick Martone is like those people in Philadelphia?'

'What?'

She repeated it.

'No. Just vicious rumors. He's a businessman, that's all. By the way, I have to go to Argentina tomorrow. A problem with the power company there. They need me. I know it's last minute but—'

'They know a good man when they see one,' she said. 'It's all right. How long will you be gone?'

'Just a couple of days.'

She came around behind and kissed his bald spot. 'I just want you to travel safe.'

'Oh, sure, I'll be fine,' he said, wondering at her change in attitude. 'I need to do a few things out in my office to get ready for the trip.'

'All right,' she said. 'But hurry back. I feel like a cuddle tonight.'

The minute he was gone from the house she called Clarence Miller III on his cell phone.

'He's going to Argentina tomorrow,' she said.

'What time, what flight?'

'I don't know, but I'll find out and let you know.'

SIXTEEN

Bill Whitlock, a special investigator for the DEA and a member of a task force involving the US Customs and Border Protection Agency, met late the next day with members of his team in his office on Army-Navy Drive, in Pentagon City, Virginia. Whitlock, who'd been with the DEA for eleven years, was one of almost five thousand agents charged with stemming the importation of drugs into the United States. An increase in trafficking across the US-Canada border, particularly with drugs emanating from Argentina, had resulted in a joint initiative with Canadian authorities. A list had been drawn up of Canadian citizens who made frequent trips to that South American country. Included on it was a former engineer at Power-Can, Carlton Smythe.

'Smythe, Carlton,' Whitlock said, reading from the dossier he held, 'fifty-three years of age, married, no children, worked at Power-Can but left more than a year ago, married into money. His father-in-law, now deceased, Walter Wiggins, was a successful venture capitalist in Toronto. Smythe has made frequent trips to Buenos Aires over the past year, including one today. Always flies First Class, stays at the same hotel, the Four Seasons.' He looked up and smiled. 'It seems that Mr Smythe has a lady friend in Buenos Aires, name Gina Ellanado, always in her company.' He tossed photographs on the table of Smythe embracing Gina at the airport and in front of 'El Beso,' the sculpture of two lovers in the Palermo Woods area of Buenos Aires.

'What's he do when he's there?' a member of the team asked, which elicited laughter. 'I withdraw the question,' he said.

'She's a knockout,' someone said.

'So he has good taste in women,' Whitlock continued. 'No evidence of any involvement with drug dealers in Argentina, but this is of interest. We started tracking him just before that photo was taken, and we've kept tabs on him in Canada. Catch this. Yesterday he flies on a private plane to a Mafia safe house outside of Philly. Guess who he was with: Dominick Martone, the don of Toronto.'

'That *is* interesting,' someone said.

'Where the turf war broke out yesterday?'

'Yup. Arnaud in Canada got the information from the outfit that charters flights out of Toronto. Seems the plane returned with a couple of bullet holes in its fuselage.'

'So what the hell is this guy Smythe doing

flying to a mob confab with Martone?'

'Good question,' said Whitlock. 'As far as we know, Martone is one of those old-school Mafioso who stays out of the drug business. We've been tracking him for years. No drug involvement that we know of.'

'Which doesn't mean that some of his lower level *goombahs* follow the rule.'

Whitlock shook his head. 'I can't see this Smythe getting involved in the drug trade,' he said. 'His wife's rolling in dough, big house in a fancy part of town, expensive cars – she drives a Jag – entrenched in Toronto society. Doesn't make sense for Smythe to get down and dirty.'

'What about this lady friend of his in Buenos Aires?'

'Not much on her, although our people there are doing some checking. All we have is that she's some sort of consultant to perfume companies.'

'Do the Philadelphia police know about Smythe and Martone attending that mob sit-down?'

'If they do, it didn't come from us. We don't need some local police department getting in the way. We'll take a closer look at this Carlton Smythe. Meantime let's move on to the next name on the list.'

Dominick Martone woke up that morning in a foul mood. His seemingly nonchalant reaction to the fracas outside of Philadelphia did not accurately reflect what he was really thinking and feeling. His view of the other two Mafia leaders at the meeting was less than sanguine. As far as he was concerned, the heads of other crime families, especially in the States, were buffoons: crude, uneducated men lacking in social graces and appreciation for the finer things in life – the arts, soaring symphonies, great paintings, classic literature, and, of course, opera, especially opera. Having to do business with them was distasteful for this aria-loving godfather.

Not that those working for him were any better, leg-breaking goons who wouldn't know Callas from Lady Gaga. He needed them, of course, but preferred the company of Toronto's more genteel set and sought it whenever possible. Recently he'd been considering quitting. He didn't need the money; he was filthy rich. The problem was that he had no one to whom to pass the baton. His two children prudently avoided any connection with their father's *real* business, although they knew that his many legitimate businesses depended upon his darker side. Martone's wife, Maria, a gourmet cook whose dishes surpassed those found in any Italian restaurant, was the rock in his life, and he often gave thanks to God for having found her.

Maybe it *was* time to quit he decided that

morning as he showered and shaved to a recording of Maria Callas singing the difficult aria *Una Voce Poco Fa* from Rossini's *The Barber of Seville* that came through twin speakers in his palatial marble bathroom, one of six in his home. He moaned with pleasure at particularly poignant moments in the aria, and had to wipe tears from his cheeks during an especially moving section.

Maria had prepared a large breakfast for him, as she always did, and he sat in a glass-enclosed atrium at a table draped with a fresh white linen tablecloth. Gleaming silverware was precisely lined up on his napkin, and a vase of freshly cut roses from their greenhouse added a splash of color.

'What do you have planned for today?' Maria asked as she poured them fresh-squeezed orange juice, and filled their coffee cups.

'Meetings,' he said, 'always meetings. Do you have a nice day planned?'

'I'm visiting Julia and the children.' Julia was married to Robert, their elder son, who managed Martone Import-Export on the outskirts of the city. 'And I must make two batches of butterscotch *biscotti* for the women's club.'

Martone laughed and smacked his lips. 'Save a few for me,' he said. Maria made the cookies, a variation on the basic Italian *biscotti*, with almonds, butterscotch chips, and bourbon. They were Martone's favorites.

After breakfast, Martone and Maria spent a half hour admiring plants and flowers in the greenhouse before Hugo and his ferret-faced companion activated the electric gates and pulled into the circular driveway. Martone kissed Maria goodbye and said he'd be home in time for dinner, a rarity.

Martone and his gang drove to a vacant warehouse in a complex he owned where some of his men had arranged a table and chairs, and a second table containing a fruit platter, Danish pastries, coffee, and a bottle of Limoncello, which Martone had specified because Vinnie Tourino, head of one of New York's five criminal families and Martone's guest that morning, was particularly fond of it.

Hugo and four others took up positions outside the warehouse. Ten minutes later a black Town Car pulled up and Tourino and three of his protectors got out.

'He's inside,' Hugo told Tourino. 'I got his weapon.'

Tourino hesitated before handing his handgun to an associate.

The New York crime chief entered the warehouse where Martone stood by the food table nibbling on a pastry. 'Hey, Vinnie,' he said, dropping the pastry and coming to greet his guest.

'You eat that stuff you get fat and soft,'

Vinnie said. He was a rugged-looking man with square features, a head of thick black hair, and a scar that ran from the corner of his right eye down to his mouth. He wore a gray suit tailored for him in London, and black tasseled loafers.

'Fat? Yeah. Soft? Never. Come, sit down. The others'll wait outside. That OK with you?'

'Sure it's OK,' Tourino said, taking a chair, crossing his legs, and pinching the already razor-sharp crease in his pants between a thumb and index finger.

'Something to eat, drink?'

'No.'

'I got Limoncello 'specially for you.'

'Let's get on with it, Dom. I got to get back to New York. I got a plane reservation in three hours. So what's this so-called deal of a lifetime you're selling?'

Martone took the second seat and fixed Tourino in a hard stare. What he saw across the table from him was the Duke of Mantua, undoubtedly one of opera's most infamous villains as created by the composer Verdi in his opera *Rigoletto*. Vinnie Tourino's reputation was that of a sadistic, barbaric enforcer, who'd worked his way up from beating payments out of loan shark debtors to head of the family.

'All right,' Martone said, 'here's the deal.' He explained it quickly and without embellishment. When he was finished, Tourino smiled. 'You really think this guy can pull this off, flip a fucking switch and kill all the juice from here to DC?'

'If I didn't think that, Vinnie, I wouldn't have put up a million bucks myself. What do you think I am, a chump?'

Tourino went through a series of stretching exercises, twisting his neck, clamping his hands behind his head, and taking deep breaths, as though they were part of his decision-making process. Martone said nothing, his thoughts vacillating between butterscotch *biscotti* and wanting to blow Tourino away.

'OK,' Tourino finally said. 'A half-mil.'

Martone laughed. 'Like I said, Vinnie, I'm no chump. It'll cost you a million, cash up front. Otherwise, no deal. Hey, Vinnie, I'm being generous am I not? I don't need New York money. I already got another five or six cities come in on the deal. So, take it or leave it. I appreciate you coming up here to listen, and no hard feelings if you pass.'

'How long the lights'll be out?'

'My expert says maybe a day, but sure as hell six, seven hours, plenty of time to hit a dozen places, more.'

'All right, Dominick, I'm in.'

'Good. You send the money through the usual channels and I give you the date and time. Nice, clean, easy deal, the way business should be.'

As Martone walked him to the door, Tourino said, 'I got a bad feeling about this, Dominick.'

Martone slapped him on the back. 'Hey, Vinnie, relax and leave everything to Uncle Dominick. Believe me, you've never made such easy money.'

While Martone and Vinnie Tourino cut their deal, Carlton Smythe passed through Customs and was in Gina Ellanado's arms in the Buenos Aires passenger terminal.

'You call me last minute,' she said as they walked arm-in-arm to baggage claim. 'You come back so soon.'

'I had to,' he said. 'I couldn't stand to be away from you another minute.'

He tried to mask his anxiety as he waited for his suitcase to come tumbling down the moving carousel. He'd hidden forty thousand dollars in amongst his clothing and prayed that it wouldn't be picked up by security machines – or dogs. He'd read that some airport security agencies used dogs not only to sniff out explosives, but cash as well. He'd sprayed the money with cologne before leaving, hoping that would screw up their scent. As his bag came into view he drew a sigh of relief. There were no dogs, and his suitcase didn't appear to have been opened.

Now that his heart had stopped racing, and he'd mopped perspiration from his brow, they went to where a row of taxis waited. Neither was aware that a man with a tiny camera had been snapping pictures of them since Smythe came off the plane. His name was Popi Domingo, and he worked for Clarence Miller III's agency in Toronto. He'd been told that Smythe always stayed at the Four Seasons, and told the next cab in line to take him there.

When Smythe and Gina arrived at the hotel, another person stood casually reading a newspaper. His name was Luis Cortez, and he worked for Bill Whitlock at the DEA. As the taxi driver pulled Smythe's luggage from the trunk, the man started photographing them and continued until they'd passed through the doors and were inside the Four Seasons.

The paparazzi had nothing on them.

SEVENTEEN

'I would like to meet your friend, the banker,' Smythe told Gina after he'd given her the forty thousand dollars and they'd made love in his suite.

He'd fixated on the 'private banker' Gina had mentioned during their last time together. Actually, he'd fixated on a number of things during the flight to Buenos Aires. The strain of the past few weeks had taken its toll.

He knew that in launching his adventure with Gina and Martone he was acting like an impetuous schoolboy, living for the moment and never stopping to consider the ramifications. As much as he tried to rationalize his actions – getting revenge on his former employer, bailing out of a loveless marriage, seeking pleasure that he'd decided he was due – the reality was that he'd put into motion a criminal act, which made him no better than Martone and others like him.

His betrayal of Cynthia weighed heavily, and he worried while flying home from his latest tryst with Gina that he might be carrying a venereal disease to his wife durng their infrequent moments together in one bed to 'cuddle', her euphemism for making love. He'd never used protection with Cynthia because she was infertile, and it didn't matter anyway because she was the only woman he'd been with since their marriage – until Gina. He hadn't had any condoms with him the first few times they'd made love, not that they would have been put to use. Their passion was so powerful and sudden that there wouldn't have been time to slip one on. He debated using a condom later in their affair but decided it would no longer matter. Gina provided her own birth control, and the idea that this perfect female creature would transmit a venereal disease was absurd.

What would the fallout be once the blackout was a reality and he'd left Cynthia and Toronto for good? The good name of Walter Wiggins would be a laughing stock when word got out about what he'd done.

Carlton Smythe, adulterer, liar, schemer, criminal, fraud, weasel: those names and worse would be forever attached to Cynthia and by extension to her prestigious family. And there was his own family who would also suffer disgrace, although his father had long been dead. His mother resided in a dementia facility and didn't know what day it was, let alone be able to react to the news that her only son was a regular John Dillinger.

But while these unpleasant thoughts swirled through his head, he kept coming back to this so-called private banker. He had two concerns about him, the least of which was whether he could be trusted with the money that Smythe, via Gina, would place in his hands. Smythe's biggest fear was that Gina and this banker were in some way romantically and sexually involved. That would be a crushing blow.

'Why do you want to meet Guillermo?' Gina asked as they sat naked in bed following their lovemaking.

'Oh, no special reason,' Smythe said. 'But if he's going to be handling our money, I think I should at least get to know him. Guillermo. That's his name?'

'Yes. Guillermo Guzman.'

'Guillermo Guzman,' Smythe repeated. 'Yes, I would like to meet him.'

'You will one day.'

'I'd like to meet him now – while I'm here,' he said, surprised that he'd stated his demand so forcefully. 'Maybe we can have dinner together. I have to leave tomorrow. I was hoping that you'd found a house to rent for when I'm here permanently.'

'I have been so busy,' she said, 'but I promise I will begin looking tomorrow.'

She got out of bed and walked naked to

the closet, pulled out one of the hotel's robes, slipped it on, and went to the living room where she made a call. Smythe stood in the doorway and listened as she spoke with the banker in rapid-fire Spanish; he understood only a word or two. She hung up and said, 'He will meet us for dinner tonight at *Casa Coupage*. It is a very fine restaurant in the Palermo district.'

'That sounds good,' Smythe said. He came up behind and wrapped his arms around her, but she moved away and disappeared into the bathroom. He pondered why she'd seemed reluctant to call the banker, but soon forgot about it after they'd made love again and dozed off, her head on his bare chest, one leg splayed across his torso.

Later, they took a taxi to Solero Street in the Palermo district of the city. Following them were two other cars. Clarence Miller III's man in Buenos Aires, Popi Domingo, occupied one, the DEA agent Luis Cortez the other.

Casa Coupage was what's known in Argentina as a 'closed door' restaurant, patterned after the *paladares* in Havana, family-owned restaurants located within private homes. The stone marble building, set in a block of equally expensive homes, didn't have a sign on the door. Smythe knocked and the heavy wooden door was opened by a uniformed waiter

'Señor Guzman has a reservation,' Gina said in Spanish.

'*Si, si*,' the waiter said. 'Please come in.'

He led them to a lovely patio garden flanked by two small dining rooms.

'Señor Guzman has not arrived yet,' they were told. Another waiter appeared with two glasses of Champagne. 'While you wait,' he said.

'Beautiful place,' Smythe said to Gina.

'Yes, very lovely.'

'You've been here before?'

'A few times.'

'With Mr Guzman?'

'Yes. It is one of his favorite restaurants in all of Buenos Aires.'

'You've talked to him about the money you will be getting from me?'

'Yes. You do not have to worry. He is a good man.'

The good man arrived a few minutes later. Smythe had the same visceral reaction as he always had with Dominick Martone: envy. Guillermo Guzman was movie-star handsome. His swarthy features, dark brown eyes – bedroom eyes as they used to be called – were large and had a dreamy quality to them. He was six feet tall and had a full head of black hair tinged with gray at the temples. He wore a white linen sport coat, teal silk shirt open at the collar revealing a tuft of black chest hair, three thin strands of gold around his neck, multiple rings, and a gold earring in his ear. Smythe had never seen teeth quite that white. Faces of famous Latin-American movie stars came and went – Ricardo Montalban, Andy Garcia, Ricky Martin, Antonio Banderas.

'Ah,' Guzman said, 'I finally get to meet the famous Mr Carlton Smythe.'

'My pleasure,' said Smythe, whose bony hand was lost in Guzman's larger one.

'Gina talks about you constantly,' Guzman said. 'You have made quite an impression on her.'

'And she on me,' said Smythe.

Guzman was brought his glass of Champagne. He toasted, 'To my new Canadian friend – and to the beautiful Gina.'

As they went to one of the dining rooms, Smythe noted that there were only four tables. Three were occupied. Lovely original oil paintings dominated the walls. The table was elaborately set with the finest napery and utensils. As he sat, he also noticed that built into the table was a light source.

'To read the menu better?' he asked.

'No, to better see the color of the red wine when it is served,' Guzman explained. 'Some stupid tourists come here and keep flicking the lights on and off.'

'I promise I won't do that,' Smythe said.

Guzman laughed heartily. 'I am certain that any man Gina falls in love with would

174

never be guilty of that.'

Smythe laughed along with him, pleased to hear those words.

Guzman offered suggestions from the menu: 'I recommend the calamari to start, then trout which they serve with apples and sauce – *magnifique!* – then the sirloin steak with a wonderful thick cheddar sauce, the white salmon, or the veal. I am sure that you will find any of those choices to be to your liking.'

It was salmon for Gina, veal for Smythe, steak for Guzman, accompanied by a bottle of Argentinean pinot noir, which soon became three bottles.

During dinner, Smythe asked Guzman what was meant by a 'private bank'?

'A good question,' Guzman said. 'Let me just say that in Argentina the government has imposed many foolish rules that keep banks from making their profits, heavy-handed regulations that stifle growth. Private banks are ... they are the refuge of the wealthy who look to preserve their wealth.'

'Are you a financial advisor?' Smythe asked.

'Oh, yes. Many of the wealthiest men in Buenos Aires put their trust in me to manage their finances. I am honored that they hold me in such high regard.'

Smythe had other questions but didn't get

to ask them as the conversation turned to less weighty subjects.

At the end of dinner Guzman didn't make a move to pay the bill, three hundred dollars in US currency, and Smythe did. Before they left, Guzman insisted that they cap off the night at a *milonga*, a tango party.

'I'm really tired after the plane ride,' Smythe said.

'And the *milonga* will awaken your body and spirit,' Guzman said. 'A visit to Argentina must always include the tango.'

They exited the restaurant and climbed into Guzman's silver Mercedes sedan. The DEA's Cortez, who was parked on the same side of the street, started his engine and fell in behind.

The Miller Agency's Buenos Aires investigator, Domingo, had to make a U-turn from his parking space on the opposite side of the street, and almost lost Guzman's Mercedes as it sped to the tango club.

The club was hopping when they arrived, the dance floor chock-a-block with dancers as Smythe, Gina and Guzman were given a table at the edge of the floor. Guzman ordered a bottle of wine. A four-piece tango band – violin, piano, bass and bandoneón – provided the pulsating, sensuous music for the many couples strutting their stuff beneath multi-colored lights.

Gina, who'd been strangely reticent during dinner, seemed energized by the scene and asked Smythe to dance.

'Oh, no,' he said. 'I'm afraid I'm not up to it tonight, dear.'

'Will I do as a partner?' Guzman asked her.

'Do you mind?' she asked Smythe.

'No, no, go ahead,' he said, stifling a yawn. The trip, the wine, the heavy meal and his mental gyrations had exhausted him. All he wanted to do was climb into bed next to her and sleep.

He fought his fatigue and watched Guzman and Gina engage on the dance floor. Guzman had explained the tango during dinner: 'It is all about the relationship between the man and the woman, a total giving of one's self to the other, an invitation to seduction.' His explanation was now being demonstrated in front of Smythe, and he wasn't pleased with the display. Guzman and Gina were wrapped around each other, dipping, gazing deeply into each other's eyes, bodies pressed together, their sweat mingling, hot breath on their necks and cheeks. Smythe squirmed with discomfort and realized how angry he'd become over the course of the evening.

'She is the perfect tango partner,' Guzman said when they returned to the table.

'Yes, I know,' Smythe said, wanting to bolt with Gina and escape this stereotypical

Latin lover with the dazzling white smile and the virility he exuded. Guzman poured wine, and he and Gina conversed in Spanish while Smythe seethed, and battled to stay awake. An hour later, Guzman paid the tab and they went to his car.

'You look like a dead man,' Guzman said as he pulled from the curb, with Cortez and Domingo providing a surreptitious two-car parade, with plenty of distance between vehicles. Neither man knew of the other, nor did Guzman realize that he'd been followed all evening. Cortez and Domingo watched from different vantage points near the Four Seasons as Smythe, Gina and Guzman got out of his Mercedes. Guzman embraced her, for too long a time as far as Smythe was concerned. He shook Smythe's hand and said, 'You are a very lucky man, Mr Smythe, to have captured this beautiful woman's heart. I look forward to when you come here to live, and I assure you that the money you bring with you will be in capable hands – mine. *Buenas noches.*'

The Miller Agency's Buenos Aires investigator, Popi Domingo, had not recognized Guzman, and didn't think anything of Smythe spending an evening with him.

But DEA Agent Cortez had. Guillermo Guzman was known in Buenos Aires as a possible money launderer for Argentinean drug cartels.

'Very interesting,' Cortez muttered as he made notes before driving away and calling it a night.

EIGHTEEN

New York crime boss Vinnie Tourino sat with Angelo, his capo, in the black BMW on the outskirts of JFK Airport, in Queens. Parked behind was a second black car containing four of Vinnie's trusted men.

'So tell me again about this guy, Angelo.'

'What can I tell you, Vinnie? He wants in on the action, wants to buy into the deal. Hell, you're already out a mil so maybe it makes sense to copper your bet.'

'Coppa?'

'Copper your bet. It's an expression. Sure, we'll probably get more than the mil back, depending on how many places we can hit once the electricity is turned off. But this guy Tengku is willing to put up a half mil for Queens. What's to lose?' Angelo giggled, which always annoyed Vinnie. 'I think we take the deal the guy is offering. Like I said, what's to lose?'

'I don't trust people like that,' Vinnie said.

'People like *what*, Vinnie?'

'Like this guy – what's his name?'

'Tengku. It's a weird name but—'

'It sure the fuck *is* weird,' Vinnie said. 'Like I said, I don't trust people like this. What's he got, only one name?'

Angelo shrugged.

'It's his first name?'

'How the fuck do I know?'

'Where you say he's from?'

'Malaysia.'

'Where's that?'

'In Asia. It's like a Chinese island.'

'Chinese? I don't trust the Chinese. Every fucking thing we buy gets made in China.'

'Yeah, I know, Vinnie. They're eating our lunch.'

'What?'

'That's like a figure of speech. It don't matter if you trust them, Vinnie. It's cash upfront, on the barrelhead.'

'On the *what*?'

'On the barrelhead. It's an expression.'

'Oh. So he wants Queens for a half million?'

'Right. I told him to bring the money with him, no second chances. He buys in now or he's out.'

They turned upon hearing a car. As it pulled up next to the BMW, Vinnie's men got out and fanned around it. The doors on the newly arrived vehicle opened and two men stepped out. One was dressed like a businessman, suit, tie, shoes polished to a high gloss. The second man wore wrinkled chino pants and a red windbreaker over a T-shirt.

Vinnie and Angelo also got out. Vinnie stared at the well-dressed man as though looking at a newly arrived alien from another planet.

'Mr Tourino?' the man in the suit said.

'Yeah. You're?'

'My name is Tengku. It is a pleasure meeting you.' He spoke with a British accent.

'Yeah, me too. You know Angelo?'

'Of course I do, sir. He is the reason we meet here today.'

'Yeah, well, let's talk.'

'Right,' said Angelo. 'Let's get down to brass tacks.'

Vinnie scowled at his capo, who shrugged.

'You are obviously a man of action,' Tengku said. 'I like that. As I am sure Angelo has explained to you, I am aware of a certain business arrangement you have entered into involving the supply of electricity.'

'That's right,' Vinnie said. 'And you want to buy in.'

'Exactly, sir.'

'You have the dough with you? A half a million?'

'Oh yes, sir, I do indeed. Do we have an understanding?'

Tourino looked at Angelo, who nodded.

'I assume, sir, that once I turn over the money I will be given the precise date and time that the cessation of electricity will occur?'

Vinnie said, 'That's right. I got it right here.' He patted his jacket's breast pocket. His million dollars had been sent by messenger to Martone in Toronto the previous night, and Martone had provided Tourino with the blackout information.

Tengku clicked his fingers at his companion, who opened the trunk of their car, brought out a bulging leather suitcase, and handed it to his boss.

'I assure you, sir, that all the money is there. Of course you are free to count it if you wish.'

'Out here, in the wind?' Vinnie said. 'Angelo vouches for you, that's good enough for me.'

'I am pleased to hear that, sir. Now, may I have the pertinent information?'

'Yeah, right.'

Tourino pulled a piece of paper from his pocket and handed it to Tengku. He looked at it, smiled, and handed it to his companion. 'It has been a pleasure doing business with you, sir.'

'Yeah, well, just remember that what you bought is Queens, no place else. *Capisci?*'

'Pardon?'

'He wants to make sure you understand,' Angelo explained. 'You bought Queens, that's it.'

'Yes, of course. Thank you. I have found this exchange to be quite pleasant.'

Vinnie's two cars drove off. Tengku went in another direction. The well-dressed Malaysian smiled, then laughed heartily. He looked up through the car's moon roof, clasped his hands, and said, 'It will be done. In your name it will be done.'

NINETEEN

The next day, DEA agent Bill Whitlock and his handpicked team met in his Pentagon City office. He'd just gotten off the phone with Antoine Arnaud of the Canadian Border Services Agency. Arnaud had been assigned to augment Whitlock's work on the Canadian side of the border and had become a valuable source of information.

'What's new on Arnaud's end?' Whitlock was asked after he'd hung up.

He adjusted his half-glasses and squinted at the notes he'd made during his phone conversation with Arnaud. 'Sometimes I can't read my own writing,' he said. 'OK, here's what he said, only I'm not sure what to make of it. Smythe, our subject of interest, used to work at the huge Canadian power plant Power-Can. While he was there he supervised a team of engineers including a French-Canadian named Paul Saison. Saison lives in Toronto with a woman named Angelique. With me so far?'

There were nods around the conference table.

'Angelique has a sister in Montreal named Celine, who happens to be engaged to Antoine.'

'Arnaud's engaged?'

'Right. According to Antoine, Saison is a bit of a buffoon, a drunk who hangs on to his job at Power-Can because of the quota system – you know, having to employ so many French-Canadians. Anyway, according to Saison's lady friend, she came back from visiting her sister and got into a scrum with Saison, which evidently isn't a rare occurrence. During their argument Saison starts boasting that he's about to become rich, mentioned a quarter of a million dollars he'll soon be getting.'

'Getting it from where?'

Whitlock shrugged. 'Antoine says his fiancée's sister didn't have any information about that. But here's what's intriguing. The sister *did* say that Saison mentioned Smythe as the one who came up with "the plan", whatever it is.'

' "The plan",' a few at the table murmured.

'That's all I've got,' Whitlock said, 'except that Saison left a scrap of paper on the table when he went to bed on which somebody had written "Friday, August twenty-two, nine forty-five pm".'

'Did this Angelique ask Saison about it?'

'Evidently not, at least from what she told

her sister. According to her, Saison left the house early the next morning and took the paper with him. I should add that Saison's girlfriend didn't call her sister to report anything. She called to make fun of Saison and his boast that he'd soon be rich.'

'Maybe it means nothing,' someone offered. 'If Saison is what Arnaud says he is, a drunk and a liar, why put any credence in what he said?'

'You're probably right,' Whitlock responded. 'Antoine says that Saison is a big talker, always saying he's going to be rich. But the fact that he's been involved with Carlton Smythe tells me that we shouldn't ignore this.'

The phone rang and Whitlock picked up.

'Bill, Luis Cortez here.'

'Buenas días,' Whitlock said. 'What've you got?'

'I spent part of yesterday and last evening with Mr Smythe. He flew in and was met by the same lovely lady. They took a taxi to the Four Seasons Hotel and holed up there for the afternoon. At night they took another taxi to a restaurant, *Casa Coupage*, very popular, very expensive. While I waited outside for them to leave, Guillermo Guzman arrived and went inside.'

'Guzman. Guzman,' Whitlock said. 'Right. Isn't he the guy you suspect is laundering Argentinean drug money?'

'One and the same. I didn't think much of it until Smythe and the lady left the restaurant. They were accompanied by Guzman. He drove them in his car to a tango nightclub. I went inside, sat at the bar, and observed. Smythe looked fatigued, didn't dance, but Guzman and the woman went at it. Guzman drove them back to the hotel, hugs all around, and that was it.'

'So Smythe and Guzman spent an evening together,' Whitlock said loud enough for others at the table to hear. 'Good work, Luis.'

'Thanks. I checked with my airline contacts. Smythe is flying back to Canada tomorrow morning.'

Luis Cortez wasn't the only one reporting in that day.

Clarence Miller III arrived at the Smythe household a little before noon.

'Please come in,' Cynthia said. 'My mother and I made sandwiches and lemonade.'

'That's very thoughtful of you,' Miller said as he followed her to the dining room where Mrs Wiggins sat regally at the head of the table.

'Good morning,' she said.

'Good morning, Mrs Wiggins. It's a lovely day.'

'Much too humid,' she said. 'You have

something to report?'

'Yes, I do.'

'Would you like something to eat?' Cynthia asked nervously. 'It's warm chicken salad. My father—'

'Mr Miller isn't here to eat,' Mrs Wiggins said sharply, 'or to hear what foods your father enjoyed. He's here to report any progress he's made in determining whether your husband has been unfaithful.'

Miller adjusted his position on the chair. He sensed that Cynthia did not want to hear that her husband, Carlton Smythe, had cheated on her, and he shared her discomfort. While the agency left him by his father provided a good living, a *very* good living in this age when marital cheating was not uncommon, he did not enjoy having to report bad news to a spouse.

'My mother is right,' Cynthia said. 'Have you learned anything new?'

Before he could answer, Cynthia quickly added, 'You mentioned that Carlton has been renting an office away from the house. Have you learned any more about that?'

Miller took the opportunity to open his briefcase and take out a sheaf of paper. He consulted one piece before saying, 'No, I do not have anything new about that situation, but I do suggest that I look further into the circumstances of it as part of my overall investigation. Before we go any further, however, I must inform you that in order to go beyond the point I've already reached, there will be additional fees.'

Cynthia looked to her mother, who smiled at Miller. 'I am sure, Mr Miller, that your father told you that money was never an object with me when I retained his services. The amount of money involved is of little consequence. What matters is that my daughter – my *only* daughter – has peace of mind regarding her husband. You do realize that this family enjoys a certain prominence in this city?'

'Of course,' Miller replied.

'Should my daughter's husband prove to be unfaithful, the impact upon our reputation would be unfortunate. What I am saying, Mr Miller, is that not only must we know whether Cynthia's husband is a scoundrel, we must then take steps to minimize the fallout.'

'You made that point very clearly, Mrs Wiggins, when I was first contacted.'

'Good. I simply wish there to be no misunderstandings. As far as learning more about why Carlton saw fit to rent an office without our knowledge and approval, please feel free to pursue any avenues you consider appropriate. Your bills will be paid in a timely fashion.'

The paper that Miller had pulled from his briefcase contained notes he'd made while sitting outside Smythe's temporary office building. He added a note, 'Proceed,' placed it back in the case, and extracted the photos taken of Smythe and Gina in Buenos Aires. Cynthia looked down at the first one, burst into tears, and fled the room.

'Please excuse my daughter, Mr Miller. She isn't very strong when it comes to adversity.'

She picked up the photos one-by-one and examined them carefully. Miller filled a glass with lemonade and sipped as she completed her perusal.

'A common-looking woman, wouldn't you say?' she said.

'My man in Buenos Aires is checking into her background, Mrs Wiggins.'

'I'm sure that it will be suitably sordid.'

She dropped the pictures on the table with an air of dismissal, as though they had soiled her hands.

'Do you have anything else?' she asked.

'Not at the moment, Mrs Wiggins. I am delving further into Paul Saison, the gentleman who used to work for Mr Smythe.'

'What about money?' Mrs Wiggins said.

'As I told you—'

'I don't mean about how much your investigation will cost,' she said sharply, causing him to wince. 'Surely conducting an immoral affair in a third-world country is costing my son-in-law a great deal?'

'Well, Argentina isn't exactly a third-world country, Mrs Wiggins.'

'Perhaps not, but you know how those people are. My question about money has not been answered.'

'I'll need information from you and Mrs Smythe to help me look into Mr Smythe's finances.'

'Whatever you need. I'll put you in touch with our accountants. He's obviously been squandering my family's money.'

Cynthia reappeared. She'd dried her eyes and had applied fresh make-up.

'I apologize,' she said, 'but to see my husband with another woman is ... well, it's devastating.'

Mrs Wiggins patted her daughter's hand. 'Of course it is, dear, but it is better to know than to suspect. I assure you that Carlton will pay for his indiscretion.'

Miller was glad to leave the Smythe house. When contacted by Mrs Wiggins to take the case, he'd reviewed his father's file that contained notes and pictures from when Walter Wiggins was the subject of the investigation. Now that he'd met the woman Mr Wiggins had cheated on, he understood why the wealthy venture capitalist had sought the softness of another woman.

But making such judgments was not what he was paid to do. Armed with carte blanche where future fees were concerned, he pulled out of the driveway and headed for the building in which Carlton Smythe had rented an office.

TWENTY

Joe Schott had been living in Buenos Aires for ten years. Two factors had led him to move there from Chicago: his contentious divorce, and the charges brought against him by the Illinois attorney general for financial fraud and for using the US mail for criminal purposes. While living in Chicago he'd concocted a real estate scheme that lured people desperate to partake in the American dream of owning a home into sub-prime mortgages. After making a hefty down payment, they were told that they'd failed to qualify, and that their deposits were non-refundable.

The Better Business Bureau got on Schott's case. The attorney general did too after having received numerous complaints. Schott and his partner were indicted, but Schott's well-connected lawyer managed to get the charges dropped in return for a hefty donation to the judge's nephew who was running for the state Senate. Simultaneously, Schott's wife of two years, a former stripper, filed for divorce and sought alimony based upon Schott's prosperous years while running the scam. That's when he decided that the US of A wasn't a good place to ply his creative endeavors and headed south to Argentina where he had a friend who put him up, and got him involved in real estate.

Schott Premier Homes was moderately successful. It focused primarily on rentals in the city, and Schott supplemented his income through side deals that allowed him to launder money through real estate transactions. One of his occasional 'partners' was Guillermo Guzman.

Shott had met Gina Ellanado when he'd rented her an apartment. The attraction between them was immediate and strong – the beautiful, sensuous Gina, the tall, handsome and smooth Joe Schott. She accepted his invitation to dinner and they commenced a torrid love affair that lasted two months until Joe took up with a lonely, wealthy widow fifteen years his senior. That's when Gina, who'd been introduced to Guillermo Guzman by Schott, started seeing the 'private banker'. That affair lasted a few months longer than her fling with Schott had, but ended the same way when Guzman, who took pride in his reputation as a 'ladies' man', found other Latin lovelies to wine, dine and bed.

For Gina these romantic relationships had been satisfying while they lasted, but the end of each left her with a burgeoning well of emptiness that seemed to deepen with each passing year. She was thirty-four, which her few female friends assured her was the prime of her life, yet their words didn't help mitigate her loneliness. She knew that she was attractive; male attention coupled with a realistic evaluation of her image in the mirror confirmed that. But beautiful women were a dime a dozen in Brazil, in any country for that matter. She'd begun to put on weight no matter how many miles she clocked on the treadmill in the small bedroom of her equally small apartment, which she'd managed to keep Smythe from visiting. Their tangled sheets were always in the hotel suite.

She often thought that if she had money, lots of money, it would ease the ache of ageing. But the fact was that she didn't have much money and never had.

Gina Ellanado was born in Bahia Blanca, a bustling port city on the Atlantic Ocean south-west of Buenos Aires. Her parents hadn't been poor, nor were they well-off. Her father had worked his entire adult life on the docks unloading the constant stream of cargo ships that came and went. It was a physically demanding job. He dropped dead one morning while part of a crew unloading grain.

Gina's mother was a conventionally pretty woman who worked on and off at shops to supplement her husband's pay, but never kept a job long enough to build up a family financial cushion.

Gina dreamed of going to one of the city's many fine universities – she excelled at math in high school – but her father's premature death and her mother's developing dementia rendered that dream impossible. Her brother, Juan, four years older, had no interest in higher education. At twenty, he traveled to the city of Rosario where he hooked up with members of the infamous Sinaloa drug cartel which specialized in setting up meth labs and distributing their potent product, mostly to the United States. He'd been there less than a year when a war broke out between rival gangs and he and two other Sinaloa gang members were gunned down on the street. His violent death destroyed what was left of his mother's already fragile mental state and she was confined to a government-financed assisted living facility in a Bahia Blanca suburb.

Gina had been told by many, including a college student who took her virginity during her senior year, that she was pretty enough to be a model. When she turned eighteen she answered an ad run by a Buenos Aires modeling agency, rode the bus to Argentina's largest city, and auditioned. It turned out that the agency was more interested in finding beautiful women to appear in its pornographic films than in hiring models. Gina didn't succumb to their promises of big paydays and continued to seek out legitimate modeling agencies. One, run by an older woman whose face had once graced the covers of leading fashion magazines, matched Gina with a cosmetics firm that began to use her in ads. But although that company ran into financial difficulties and closed its doors, Gina had enjoyed enough exposure to be retained by a competitor, not as a model but as a consultant to its product line. It wasn't steady work or pay, nor did it provide enough money to splurge except on special occasions. But it had been sufficient to sustain what would be considered by most to be a modest, albeit comfortable lifestyle.

And then she met Carlton Smythe.

Carlton Smythe.

A man with enough money to support her as she advanced in years.

'Good to see you again, Gina,' Schott said after she had walked into his real estate office and they'd exchanged preliminary pleasantries, including kisses on the cheek. 'It's been a while. Please, sit. What brings you here this morning?'

'I am looking to rent a house.'

'Your apartment getting too cramped?'

'Yes, that's it. I would like something bigger.'

'How about a bigger apartment? I have some wonderful deals here in the city, some with balconies.'

'No, no, I would like a small house, a cottage, something outside of the city.'

He sat back, folded his hands on his chest, and said, 'This is for you and your American boyfriend?'

'*Qué?*'

'This American you've been seeing.'

'He is ... he is a Canadian. A very nice man.'

'Yeah, I'm sure he is. American, Canadian, all the same.'

'How do you know about him?'

'Guillermo called me this morning, said that you and your boyfriend went tango dancing last night.'

'It is none of your business what I do.'

He came forward and extended his palms. 'OK, OK, let's see what I have that's available.'

He opened a large book containing photos of properties he represented, found the page he was looking for, and showed it to her. 'Real pretty little place, a half hour outside of town.'

The two color photographs were of a

white stone cottage with red shutters, a red door, and a small, neatly tended rose garden in front augmented by window boxes overflowing with purple and yellow flowers. The cottage sat on a rise; the pictures had been taken on a pristine day, the vivid blue sky and a few puffy white clouds dressing up the setting.

'It looks beautiful,' she said.

'It *is* beautiful,' he said, 'small but certainly larger than your apartment. You ah ... you have enough money for upfront rent and a security payment?'

'Yes, of course I do. Is it also for sale?'

He nodded. 'You can rent it with an option to buy, or you can buy it outright.'

'I would like to rent and maybe buy one day.'

'Good. Want to see it?'

'Very much I would like to see it.'

'Then let's go.'

They drove east in his metallic green BMW convertible, the top down, the rushing air and sun on her face. Behind them in a nondescript gray sedan was Popi Domingo, Clarence Miller III's man in Buenos Aires. He'd followed Gina to Schott's office that morning and had decided to devote the day to keeping tabs on her.

After a half hour, Schott turned onto a narrow road lined with tall, graceful trees and came to a stop in front of the cottage.

Popi continued past them until his car was no longer visible. He parked, got out, and sat on a stone fence from where he could just see the cottage's front door through the trees in the viewfinder of his camera.

'It is even more pretty than in the pictures,' Gina told Schott while taking photos with a small point-and-shoot camera.

'I knew you'd like it. Come on inside. I have the key.'

The cottage's interior was every bit as lovely as the exterior, and was larger than it had seemed from outside. Windows at the rear in the two bedrooms afforded an unencumbered view of hills against the horizon. The kitchen featured updated appliances, and a sizable dining area held a long French pine table with six cane chairs.

Schott led Gina out a rear door to a covered brick terrace with table and chairs, and a small barbeque grill. Gina took a series of pictures of the terrace and the views from it.

'What do you think?' Schott asked.

'It is beautiful, *muy hermoso*. How much each month?'

Schott flashed a wide smile. 'For you, sweetheart, only six thousand Argentine *pesos*.'

'In Canadian money?'

'Let's see, about twelve hundred a month.

Three months' rent in advance, two months' security, and my commission.'

'Your commission? The owner, he does not pay you?'

'I get it from both sides, Gina. Hey, a guy has to make a living. Why do you ask about Canadian money? Your Canadian sugar daddy is paying for this?'

'I will pay in that money,' she said angrily. 'Cash.'

His eyes widened. 'Sure, but mind if I ask where you came up with all this *cash*?'

'It is none of your concern.'

'OK, I get it. Come on. We'll go back to the office and do the paperwork.'

On their way back through the cottage he attempted to pin her against a wall and kiss her, which she resisted.

'Can't blame a man for trying,' he said, not pressing the issue. 'Your love life with the Canadian must be good these days.'

'My love life is very good,' she said. 'Drop me off at my apartment. I will get the money and bring it to you at your office.'

'It's a deal,' he said. 'Sure you don't want to try out the bed, sort of christen it, you know, like a bed warming, for old times?'

'I will bring you the money, Joseph. And do not touch me again.'

They rode in stony silence back to Gina's apartment where Schott dropped her off. A half hour later she emerged from her building and hailed a taxi. Popi Domingo dutifully followed. After leaving Schott's building with the signed lease in-hand, she went to a car rental service and rented a two-door Subaru on a monthly lease. Now that she had the cottage, she intended to spend as much time there as possible, making the car a necessity.

She was feeling good.

Gina had accompanied Smythe to the airport that morning for his flight back to Toronto. She assured him that she would look at houses to rent once he was gone, and that she would send pictures of what she'd found.

As he sat in First Class of the 747 and drank a glass of Malbec red wine and nibbled on beef empanadas with black bean dipping sauce, he was surprised at the foul mood he'd taken to bed with him the night before, and that had lingered into this new day. He tried to sort out his negative feelings, to identify the reason for them. What was most upsetting was that he harbored them in the first place.

He knew of course that the evening spent with Gina's handsome friend, Private Banker Guillermo Guzman, was at the root of his discontent. Although he had been the one to ask to meet the private banker, sharing Gina with him had been tortuous at best, especially at the tango club where they seemed to be putting on a show of lust while dancing. Sure, he knew that the tango was a sensual dance and that maybe he was overreacting to their passionate embraces on the dance floor. What counted was that it was he, Carlton Smythe, who'd shared the bed with her when the night was over.

Still...

He'd considered asking Gina that morning whether she'd ever slept with Guzman but didn't, afraid that it would paint him as insecure. But the unstated question had lingered with him since waking. He couldn't shake it.

He also became consumed as the flight winged northward about packaging and getting the money to Gina. He would have preferred to deal only with her, but knew that he needed someone with knowledge of Argentina's banking system. That Guzman was, as he put it, a 'private' banker said to Smythe that he was probably engaged in shady financial dealings, which was, after all, what Smythe was engaged in himself. He had to trust Gina and her smarmy go-between. He didn't have a choice.

He decided that the next day he would collect boxes from the various shipping services and send off the bulk of the money – and keep his fingers and toes crossed that it would end up with its intended recipient.

It was another choice over which he had no control.

Becoming a criminal wasn't easy.

TWENTY-ONE

Tengku, the well-dressed gentleman from Malaysia who'd paid for the blackout franchise for Queens, NY, sat in his suite at a New York hotel with four other men. He was in an expansive mood.

'That stupid man, Tourino,' he said in his cultured, somewhat exaggerated accent. 'A baboon. It was so easy to get what we wanted from him, like taking candy from a baby.'

'Yes, a baboon,' someone said through a laugh.

'Queens he sold us,' someone else said, also laughing. 'Queens!'

'You have the report from Awrang in Washington?' Tengku asked a colleague.

'Yes, Tengku. I spoke with him an hour ago. It is better than we even imagined.'

Tengku ordered one of the men to open another bottle of white wine that had been brought to the suite by room service. An assortment of Chinese delicacies had also been delivered from a nearby restaurant. It had all the appearance of a celebratory party, which it was.

Tengku had been born in Malaysia's capital Kuala Lumpur but received his secondary education in London. He returned home to start an export business and became wealthy, shipping tin, rubber and palm oil around the world. His family was Muslim – over fifty per cent of Malaysia's population practices that faith – and Tengku's mother and father were deeply religious. Tengku was, too, in his youth, but as he grew older his involvement with religion became more political than spiritual. He grew increasingly rabid about Israel and its treatment of Palestinians, and began to thrust himself and his views into Malaysia's political life. It wasn't enough for him that the Malaysian government refused to recognize Israel and did not have diplomatic relations with the Jewish state. Tengku railed against the Jewish settlements and harsh laws impacting Palestinians, and supported a worldwide jihad. He became a vocal thorn in the side of Malaysian leaders and their British-styled parliamentary form of government which ensured freedom of religion for all citizens despite its Muslim majority.

Fed up with what he considered his government's too moderate stance, he took the millions he'd made through his company and returned to London where he became active in recruiting young Arabs to his philosophy. After the British authorities placed him under scrutiny, he moved again, this time to New York City where his views, and money, were welcomed by a small group of like-minded Islamists who'd formed an enclave in the borough of Queens.

'Tell me what Awrang says,' Tengku said.

Awrang, a young, well-educated Arab-American, was a staffer in Washington for New York Senator Miles Quinlin, the front-runner in the Democratic primary currently underway. Quinlin was an ardent supporter of Israel, championed its stance in the Israeli-Palestinian conflict, and backed any bill that provided increased military aid. That he might become the Democratic candidate for president, and probably win the White House, was anathema to Tengku.

Quinlin had to be stopped.

'Awrang says that Senator Quinlin will be in New York on the twenty-second for a fundraiser at the NY Hilton Hotel. I have his itinerary.'

The colleague handed it to Tengku, who smiled as he read it. Miles Quinlin, among many attributes, was known to be a stickler for organization. He was never late to events, and each one was meticulously planned, the schedule mapped out to the minute.

'He speaks in the ballroom at eight forty-five,' Tengku read from the sheet of paper, 'and is scheduled to conclude his remarks at nine ten. He will spend forty minutes shaking hands with those in attendance, and then be escorted to his car at nine forty. Perfect!'

'Yes, perfect,' his colleagues agreed.

For Tengku, assassinating Senator Quinlin had progressed from a fervent wish to reality after meeting Angelo, Vinnie Tourino's capo. Once Tourino had decided to buy into the deal through Dominick Martone, he'd charged Angelo with seeking out others to whom they could sell pieces of the New York franchise. Tengku and Angelo had become friendly through a bar they both frequented – although Tengku still considered himself a Muslim, he enjoyed his wine.

One night, Angelo told his Malaysian friend that there was a 'business opportunity' in which Tengku might be interested. Tengku listened carefully as Angelo sketched out for him in general terms what was involved. Tengku had no interest in using the blackout to rob anyone, but he did see it as presenting an opportunity to carry out his assassination of Senator Quinlin. Eventually he agreed to buy into the franchise by paying for the exclusive right to the borough of Queens. Queens! What he cared about was midtown Manhattan and the

Hilton Hotel where Quinlin would be attending the fundraising dinner.

On Friday, August twenty-second, 2014, the lights in the hotel and on the street would go dark. Mayhem would ensue. And Tengku's followers would see to it that this evil senator and potential president of the United States would not be alive to ever support Israel again.

TWENTY-TWO

Smythe returned from his latest trip to Buenos Aires on Monday night, August eighteenth.

On Tuesday morning he awoke with a headache and sour stomach. He considered staying in bed, but there was much to be accomplished. Four days to go before the blackout and he'd be gone from Toronto for good.

The change in Cynthia's demeanor had begun to concern him. Of course at that point he'd become increasingly paranoid, and reminded himself not to read anything into her pleasant behavior. The same held true about his jealousy of Gina and Guillermo Guzman. He wondered if he was falling apart and couldn't go through with the plan.

Stop it! he told himself over and over. *Keep your eye on the goal and let nothing deter you.*

Cynthia and her mother announced at breakfast that they were going on a shopping expedition and wouldn't be back until dinner. Smythe wished them well, hiding his glee at their absence. He showered, dressed casually, and set out to visit the shipping companies he'd decided to use to transport the money to Argentina. After four hours of driving and collecting the proper size boxes, he went to his rented office and brought the boxes inside. As he passed through the lobby the receptionist said, 'Mr Smythe, there was a gentleman asking for you.'

'Oh? Who?'

'He didn't leave his name. He said that he was an old friend.'

'He didn't leave his name?'

'No. He was a chatty sort, wanted to know how long you'd had your office here, that sort of thing. He asked if he could wait in your office for you but I told him I wasn't authorized to unlock your door.'

'That's a ... yes, that was a sound decision. Thank you.'

'He said he'd be back.'

Despite his determination not to allow paranoia to get the better of him, it had now returned in full force. *What* old friend? Whoever he was wanted to wait in his office? *Who* would ask that? *Why* would he ask that? He said that he'd be back? *When?* He had a fleeting recollection of a journalism course he'd taken while an undergraduate in which he was taught the five Ws of writing a lead paragraph. The only one lacking in this real-life scenario was *where?*

He checked his email. Gina had sent him photos of the cottage. They made him smile as he envisioned the two of them sitting on the terrace after making love, exotic drinks in hand, the sun setting, unlimited bliss.

But his reverie was shortlived. The thought of someone visiting his rented office and claiming to be an old friend took center stage again as he began putting together the shipping boxes and preparing mailing labels. Once the boxes were constructed, he parceled out the packs of hundred dollar bills and allotted them to their respective boxes. He withheld the two hundred and fifty thousand dollars he was to pay Saison, less what he'd advanced him, placed those bills in a plain cardboard box on which he wrote Saison's name, and shoved it beneath the desk. He also kept out a hundred thousand dollars which he intended to carry with him when he fled Toronto.

During his morning rounds he'd stopped in a department store and bought a wheeled suitcase, and another can of cologne to spray on the bills to be shipped. He'd also visited a used bookstore and purchased two dozen paperbacks. The money was sandwiched in between magazines and newspapers, with the paperback books forming a top layer. He meticulously taped the boxes shut, and wrote the addresses on the labels, believing that handwritten labels were less likely to garner attention than printed ones. The next step was to fill in the shipping documents, which he did with great care. 'Books' was entered where a description of each box's contents was required.

The chore completed, he closed his eyes and drew a deep breath. Momentarily calmer, he began to carry the boxes out to his car. He glanced nervously around the parking lot in search of someone who might have been the 'old friend' who'd stopped by. A man sat in an exterminator truck but it couldn't be him. Satisfied that he wasn't being observed, Smythe completed loading the car and headed for the same shipping companies where he'd gotten the boxes. The thought of handing over so much money to strangers had a stranglehold on his emotions, but he kept going until the last box had been dropped off, weighed, and the shipping costs paid for in cash. He'd chatted up the personnel behind the desk at each stop: 'I collect books for libraries in poor neighborhoods in Argentina,' he said. 'It's my wife's favorite charity.'

'What a wonderful thing,' he was told.

'Yes,' he replied, keeping his voice calm, 'reading is so important, especially for poor kids hoping to make a better life for themselves.'

'The world needs more people like you and your wife'

'Thank you. That's very kind.'

Clarence Miller III had followed Smythe as he made his rounds, using the black sedan that had also been parked at the office building. He stayed with him until Smythe pulled into the driveway of his home in Toronto's tony Rosewood section. Miller parked a block away and called his colleague Janet Kudrow to relieve him until midnight when it was assumed that Smythe would stay put for the rest of the night.

Miller's man in Buenos Aires, Popi Domingo, had emailed photos of Gina with Joe Schott, along with two quick pictures he'd snapped of the cottage they'd visited. Miller had replied to Domingo and suggested that he find out whether the woman would be moving into that cottage. 'Pay the real estate guy for the info if you have to,' Miller had written.

His visit to the building in which Smythe had his office hadn't borne fruit, but he hadn't really expected that it would. The next item on his agenda was to find out more about Smythe's friend, the French-Canadian Paul Saison. He'd decided that since money wasn't an object he might as well pull out all the stops and run up the bill.

Bill Whitlock and an assistant had flown to Toronto that same day to meet with their

Canadian counterpart, Antoine Arnaud.

'What's new with Carlton Smythe?' Whitlock asked the French-Canadian.

'Not much. I assigned someone to follow him this morning but some panel truck pulled in front of him and he lost him. I don't know where he is at the moment.'

'Paul Saison?' Whitlock asked after consulting a piece of paper.

'Still checking into his background,' Arnaud replied. 'No criminal record, married and divorced twice although there's a question whether his second marriage was legal, big gambler at the racetrack, frequents strip clubs, a boozer, has a live-in girlfriend, Angelique.'

'A sterling character,' Whitlock's assistant said.

'No connections between him and drug runners or the mob?' Whitlock asked.

'No,' Arnaud replied.

'So his meeting with his ex-boss might be nothing more than former colleagues getting together.'

'Fair assumption,' said Arnaud, 'except for what his girlfriend told her sister, my fiancée, Celine.'

Whitlock consulted his paper again. 'Nine forty-five. Friday, August twenty-second. That's what was on the note his girlfriend found?'

'Right.'

'Anything special happening on that date here in Canada, a holiday or something?'

'No.'

'What about Saison's girlfriend? Think interviewing her would result in anything?'

'There's no reason for her to talk to us,' Arnaud said. 'I think we can get more information through what she tells her sister.'

'Your fiancée,' Whitlock said, smiling. 'Congratulations, Antoine.'

'Thanks. I just hope that Angelique doesn't do anything stupid like marrying Saison. I'd hate to have him for a brother-in-law.'

Saison had called in sick that day and spent the afternoon at the Woodbine race track where he picked losers in every race. He left the track and used what money was left in his pocket to buy two burgers at a fast-food outlet and to have a drink at a strip club not far from his apartment.

He was pleased that Angelique wasn't there when he returned home. He uncorked a bottle of cheap Pinot Noir and was swigging from it when the phone rang. He checked his Timex watch and had to squint to read the time through the heavily scratched lens. Eight o'clock.

'Paul, it's Carlton.'

'Oh, Smythe, my friend. You at home with your rich wife?'

'Yes. Actually I'm in my office in the back.

Is your lady friend there?'

'No. Why? You want to speak with her?'

'No, I want to speak with you. We're getting close to the date.'

'Ha! You think I would forget something like that?'

'No, I ... Paul, we should get together for one last time to make sure we haven't forgotten anything. Also, I've come up with a plan how to give you your money *after* you've created the blackout.'

'That is something to talk about, Smythe. You want to meet now?'

'No, tomorrow, before you start your night shift.'

'I work in the day tomorrow.'

'What? Paul, we only have a few days before the blackout. You have to be working at night.'

'I know, I know. On Thursday I work at night, and on Friday, too.'

Smythe's sigh of relief could be heard on Saison's end.

'Smythe? You there?'

'Yes, I'm here. We'll meet at that Chinese restaurant where I picked you up last time.'

'No, no, Smythe. I don't like Chinese food, the drinks they are terrible. We meet someplace else where they know how to make drinks. I meet you at Le Papillon, on Front Street, the best French food in Toronto.'

'That's very public, Paul. We'd be better off—'

'Hey, my sweetie-pie just walked in. Tomorrow night, six thirty, Le Papillon, *oui*?'

Saison hung up.

Smythe silently cursed the French-Canadian. Were he able, he would have severed him from the plan, but he knew that such an act was impossible. He would have to meet him at Le Papillon in Toronto's Old Town and hope that he wouldn't run into anyone there that he knew.

Friday, August twenty-second suddenly seemed years away.

TWENTY-THREE

The following morning, Wednesday, Gina Ellanado drove to the cottage in her rented Subaru and spent two hours relaxing in its various rooms, and on the terrace. She was deep in thought as she basked in its serenity.

She'd had dinner the previous night with Guillermo Guzman, who wanted to go over with her the plans for the money that was to arrive at his office Friday morning.

'You are sure that the authorities will not confiscate it?' Gina asked as they dined on rib-eye steaks and salads at Cabaña Las Lilas, one of Buenos Aires' finest *parrillas*, a grill restaurant, located near the docks at Puerto Madero.

Guzman flashed one of his brightest smiles, the one he used to put prospective clients for his financial advice at ease. 'Gina, my sweet, you worry too much. As I've told you, I have friends in the government that look the other way when I receive a shipment of *anything*, including large sums of money.'

The smile she returned was half-hearted.

'So tell me, Gina, where does this money come from?'

'From my friend in Canada.'

'Yes, I know that, but where does he come up with a million dollars in cash?'

'He is a businessman. He has been working on a very big deal and—'

'Big deals don't get paid in cash, Gina.'

'You ask me questions I do not have the answer for.'

'Look,' he said as he savored another bite of his incredibly tender *ojo de bife* from cattle personally raised and butchered by the restaurant, 'I know that you've latched on to this sugar daddy from Canada who—'

Her eyes flashed anger. 'I know what that means, Guillermo, and I do not like it. Carlton is a good and decent man who loves me.'

'A good and decent *rich* man.'

'Is it so terrible that a man I have met and who is in love with me also happens to be rich?'

'Of course not. But you keep saying that he's in love with you. Are you in love with *him*?'

Gina didn't feel she had any choice but to say that she was, although it did not represent certainty. The truth was that Carlton Smythe wasn't the sort of man a hot-blooded Argentinean woman would find physically attractive. He was skinny and

pale, and while his lovemaking was ener-
getic, it lacked the raw masculinity that
she'd experienced with previous Argentinean lovers, men like Guillermo Guzman,
and others.

But Smythe possessed qualities lacking in
those other men. With the others she was
always aware that their primary concerns
were for themselves, not her. Smythe on the
other hand genuinely cared about her, and
wanted above all else to make her happy.
And, he had money. Was it sinful for her to
include his pocketbook among his attributes? She'd been raised a Catholic, although she had not regularly attended Mass
in years. Was her infatuation with Smythe's
money a sign of greed? She hoped not. She
wanted to consider herself a good person,
with proper, moral instincts.

'Dessert?' Guzman asked. 'The profite-
roles *au chocolat* here are the best.'

She thought of the extra weight around
her midsection and declined. He ordered it
for himself.

He drove her to her apartment.

'The money will be here Friday,' she said
as she prepared to get out of the car after
declining his suggestion that he accompany
her inside for a nightcap.

'You know that I'll be taking my commission for handling it,' he said.

'How much commission?'

'It's usually fifteen per cent, but this is a big deal. Lots of risk. Twenty per cent.'

'If that is what it must be,' she said. 'What must I do?'

'Nothing, Gina, just lay back and enjoy it.'

The meaning of his caustic comment was lost on her.

Now, as she sat on the terrace of the cottage that she would soon share with Smythe, the conflicting thoughts that had bombarded her drifted away with the breeze that cooled her lovely face and caused a mobile of hanging metal rods to jingle, their sound reminding her of church bells. He'd called Smythe a sugar daddy, which had rankled her. What was his friend, Joe Schott's wealthy, wrinkled widow-lover? A sugar mommy? She smiled at having thought of that.

'Mrs Carlton Smythe,' she said aloud as she stood, took another loving glance at the scene from the terrace, and headed for her car. 'It is good.'

TWENTY-FOUR

After calling Saison from his pool house office the previous night, Smythe and Cynthia watched television until eleven. She'd spent a considerable amount of money shopping with her mother that day and had modeled her purchases for her husband, who was appropriately admiring.

'Tomorrow's opening should be special,' she told him during a commercial break.

'What opening?'

'Of *Don Giovanni*, silly.'

'Oh, right, I've been so busy I forgot.'

'The entire run is already sold out,' she said. 'It's one of my favorite operas.'

'Yes, you've said that.'

'Check your tux, Carlton. You want to look your very best.'

He spent much of the next day in his office inside the house handling family financial matters, but found concentrating to be impossible. He checked the clock on the wall every five minutes, but the red hands never seemed to move across the white face. It was as though time had stood still, and he

224

thought of old black-and-white movies in which the passage of time was indicated by calendar pages rapidly flipping across the screen. It was coming down to the wire, D-Day, when he would take a Herculean leap into a new life that was at once bright and sunny, and treacherously dark.

He napped that afternoon. When he got up, he told Cynthia that he had a dinner meeting with a potential client.

'Who?' she asked.

'A start-up tech firm,' he lied.

'Here in Toronto?'

'Yes.'

'That's good, Carlton. No traveling.'

'Yes, I don't want to travel anymore.'

'Mother will be so pleased.'

'That's good.'

'I'm pleased, too.'

Saison had dressed better than usual for dinner with Smythe at Le Papillon. He wore a wrinkled blue sport jacket over a white shirt, and his chino pants were relatively free of stains. He'd arrived early and was on his second bourbon on the rocks when Smythe walked in.

'You don't look so good, Smythe,' he said after they'd been shown to a corner table near a window.

'I feel fine,' Smythe said, nervously surveying the handsome brick-walled room in search of familiar faces.

'Have a drink, huh? I see little nerve ends sticking out of your head.'

'Don't be silly. Yes, I will have a drink.'

'So,' Saison said, 'we get close to the big money, huh?'

'Yes. We're almost there. I wanted to outline for you how you'll get your money once the blackout has occurred.'

Saison held up his index finger. 'One minute, Smythe.' He waved over the waiter and ordered an expensive bottle of Cabernet and *crepes bretonnes*. 'Oh,' he said as the waiter turned to leave, 'and some *escargots en croute* … OK, Smythe, I am listening.'

Smythe looked around before pulling a sheet of paper from his jacket pocket that he'd prepared earlier in the day. He unfolded it and placed it in front of Saison.

'So what is this, huh?'

'A drawing of my property.'

'What, you want to sell me your house?' His laugh was annoying.

Smythe took a breath to calm himself. 'I want to show you how and where you will get your money after the blackout.'

'OK, Smythe, show me.'

Smythe used a butter knife from the table to point to things on the paper. 'This is a sketch of my backyard. See? Here's the house and its back door to the yard. Here's the pool. See over here? That's a gate that leads into the yard from the street.'

'So where's the money, Smythe?'

'OK,' Smythe said, sitting back as their wine and food was delivered. When the waiter walked away, Smythe leaned closer to Saison again. 'Here's what I've worked out, Paul. On the night of the blackout there will be a party at my house. I'll be there. But you mustn't come to the house. You understand?'

'Yeah, sure.'

'A few minutes before nine forty-five I'll go out and unlock the door to the pool house.' He pointed to it again with the butter knife. 'Your money will be just inside the door in a box with your name on it. You come into the yard through the back gate, go to the pool house, open the door, take the box with the money, and leave immediately. Right?'

'You go to a party the night we do this?' Saison said, incredulous.

'Yes, of course. If I were to leave Toronto before the blackout, people would suspect that I had something to do with it. I plan to leave a few days later.' His First Class airline reservation to Buenos Aires was for Sunday, two days after the blackout.

Saison dug into the crepes and escargots as though he hadn't eaten in days. Smythe watched with disgust as the French-Canadian dribbled juice on the paper with the sketch, and wiped his mouth with the back of his hand.

'Have some, Smythe. Good escargots, best in the city.'

Smythe half-heartedly ate. The waiter reappeared to take their order for entrées, filet mignon for Saison, salmon for Smythe.

'Let's go over it one more time, Paul,' Smythe said. 'You create the blackout at nine forty-five. You come to my house, park on the road, come through the gate into my yard, open the pool house door, take the box with the money, and leave immediately. Right? *Compris?*'

'Sure, sure, I understand. You don't speak good French, Smythe.'

'Just as long as it's clear to you.'

Saison put the sketch in his pocket and they finished dinner, with Saison topping it off with *crème brulee* and a shot of aquavit.

'Careful driving home, Paul,' Smythe said as they stood in the parking lot.

He watched Saison drive from the lot and disappear down the street. 'Don't let me down, Paul,' he said aloud as he got behind the wheel and headed home. 'Just don't let me down.'

Janet Kudrow had followed Smythe to the restaurant. She took telephoto shots of the two men saying goodbye in the parking lot, and had photographed Saison's license plate. She watched Smythe pull into his driveway which snaked around the house, and park next to a blue Jaguar. She called Miller, who told her to send him the pictures and to go home, which she was glad to hear. A favorite show was on TV that she didn't want to miss.

TWENTY-FIVE

Toronto's Richard Bradshaw Amphitheatre at the Four Seasons Centre for the Performing Arts was aglow on Thursday night for the premiere of Mozart's *Don Giovanni*. As Cynthia and Smythe entered, he immediately saw among the throng of opera-goers Dominick Martone chatting with a half-dozen people, with Hugo and his skinny pal standing guard. He'd hoped that the Mafia don wouldn't be there that night, but since he was he had no choice but to acknowledge him.

'Ah, Mr and Mrs Smythe,' Martone said as they approached. 'A special night in Toronto.'

'Good evening, Mr Martone,' Cynthia said, accepting his outstretched hand. Smythe, too, shook hands with him.

'How are you, Mr Smythe?' Martone asked.

'Me? Oh, I'm fine, just fine. And you?'

'Couldn't be better.'

'Is Mrs Martone with you?' Cynthia asked.

'Unfortunately not. Maria is feeling under the weather.' He lowered his voice to a conspiratorial level. 'Besides, *Don Giovanni* isn't her favorite opera.' He laughed. 'She hates the character of Don Giovanni so much that the last time we saw it I was afraid she'd jump on the stage and personally rip out his immoral, cheating heart.'

Cynthia laughed. Smythe swallowed hard

Cynthia was called away by another board member.

'Everything set?' Martone asked Smythe in a tone that promised terrible things if it wasn't.

Smythe nodded. 'Yes, Dom, everything's set. Excuse me.'

He went to the men's room where he thought he might throw up. He splashed cold water on his face before finding his wife, who was being interviewed by a local music critic about future plans for COC. He waited until she was finished and accompanied her into the theater where choice seats were reserved for board members.

'Are you still talking with Dominick Martone about doing business with him?' she whispered in his ear.

'Ah, no, not anymore.'

'Good. I don't think he's the sort of man you should be involved with. Not that I don't adore him for his support of COC. It's just that—'

231

The lights dimmed and the orchestra began its overture.

Sitting through an opera about the rapist, murderer, thrill-seeking, morally bankrupt Don Giovanni, who allowed his sexual drive to corrode his soul, was excruciating for Smythe, and when the vile cad was stabbed in the heart by a woman he'd sexually abused, then thrown out a window and accompanied to Hell by the rotting corpse of someone he'd murdered, Smythe felt that he was about to faint.

The audience jumped to its feet and gave the cast a rousing ovation. Smythe remained in his seat until Cynthia punched him on the shoulder and gave him a withering look.

A lavish cocktail party followed the production, and the evening would be extended back at the Smythe household for a select group of friends. Voices rang out throughout the house as wannabes did their version of operatic karaoke. By the time Smythe got into bed it was after two, and he wondered when he woke up whether he would be stabbed in his heart, then tossed through the window into the garden, where Cynthia and her mother waited with hatchets. That nightmare continued throughout the night, and he awoke the next morning, Friday, August twenty-second, drenched in sweat.

TWENTY-SIX

Senator Miles Quinlin, frontrunner in the Democratic primary for president, rolled into Manhattan Friday morning with his entourage. It would be a day packed with fundraising events, culminating with a dinner at the Hilton Hotel that would add a few million dollars to his campaign coffers.

While Quinlin and his staff settled in their suite on the twelfth floor, Tengku and his small band of assassins ordered room service to their suite one floor below.

It was a bright, sunny day in New York City.

The forecast for that evening was for clear weather.

The weather forecast in Toronto for Friday, August twenty-second was for overcast skies, with an eighty per cent chance of showers and thunderstorms later in the day and into the evening.

For Carlton Smythe the forecast was for hurricane-force winds of anxiety and a deluge of emotions.

He went through the motions of helping Cynthia plan for that evening's party. He was pleased with the rainy forecast. It would keep guests from straying out into the gardens where Saison would be showing up to collect his money.

At noon, Smythe ran by his rented office where he picked up the box with Saison's name on it and brought it to the pool house, using the gate to enter the yard so as to not be seen by Cynthia or others in the main house. After locking the pool house door, he spent the rest of the afternoon doing what he could to ready the house for the arrival of guests. The caterers showed up at five and took over the kitchen, while Cynthia made multiple forays to issue last-minute instructions about the food and how she wanted it presented by the two uniformed waitresses.

Smythe was showered and dressed by six. Cynthia descended the staircase at six forty-five wearing a new purple-and-white dress she'd bought while shopping with her mother. Mrs Wiggins occupied the largest chair in the living room where she read that day's newspaper, half-glasses perched low on her aquiline nose, her eyes peering over them now and then to check on progress.

Guests began arriving at seven fifteen, greeted by Smythe and Cynthia at the door. A CD compilation of famous arias oozed from speakers in every room, and the volume of chatter increased with each arriving couple. It took every ounce of willpower for Smythe to assume a pleasant, relaxed demeanor, and to not look at his watch every thirty seconds.

The time passed with agonizing slowness.

Paul Saison's shift at Power-Can started at four that afternoon and ran until midnight. He arrived at work late, having stopped at a dive bar outside the plant to fortify himself with shots of vodka. Until that day he hadn't allowed the seriousness of what he was about to do, and the potential ramifications, to set in. Now, the only thing that kept him moving forward was the thought of a quarter-million dollars sitting in the pool house in back of Carlton Smythe's home.

Although he'd contemplated leaving Toronto and flying to Paris once he'd tripped the right switches to cause the blackout, he hadn't made any concrete plans and realized that he'd better do it now. Without a credit card – his Visa and MasterCard accounts had been closed for lack of payment – making an advance reservation would be difficult, if not impossible, so he decided simply to go to the airport once he had the money and take the next Paris flight, carrying with him only the bare necessities. He wouldn't tell Angelique that he was leaving. The hell with her. He, Paul

Saison, deserved better, and he envisioned himself lounging in bed with Parisian paramours who knew how to treat a man, and who would appreciate his many charms.

Before leaving the apartment, he'd checked his watch against the time on his alarm clock. It was running two minutes slow, and he adjusted it to coincide with the bedside digital clock.

By nine o'clock the party at the Smythe house was in full gear. Liquor flowed freely, and conversations were spirited, and loud.

'You still have that client in Argentina?' Smythe was asked by a partygoer.

'Yes, I do. Keeps me hopping, that's for sure.'

The questioner's wife said, 'It must be exhausting traveling there so often. I know that Cynthia misses you when you're away.'

'And I miss her, but business is business.'

A sudden clap of thunder caused everyone to stop talking and to look through windows.

'The weather forecasters got it right for a change,' someone said.

'Looks like it's about to pour any minute,' said another. 'I hope we don't lose power.'

'Lose power?' Smythe said, startled. 'Oh, yes, let's hope that doesn't happen. Will you excuse me?'

He moved slowly in the direction of the

kitchen and its back door leading to the yard. He didn't want to go to the pool house in a downpour and have to explain why he was wet. Mrs Kalich saw him enter the kitchen but said nothing as she continued helping the catering staff prepare platters to be passed. He reached the door, waited until he was certain that no one was paying attention, opened it and slipped outside. A brilliant flash of white sky-to-ground lightning preceded another explosion of thunder as he stepped off the patio and made for the pool house. He stopped after only a few steps. A couple embraced behind a tall bush.

'Oops,' Smythe said as he skirted the bush and continued to the small structure at the far end of the pool. He removed the key from his pocket, unlocked the door, stepped inside, used his foot to push Saison's box of money closer to the door, exited, and ran back to the house just as the rain came down in torrents.

'You're wet,' Mrs Wiggins said when he rejoined the guests.

'What? Oh, yes, I am. I ah ... I wanted to check on the outdoor furniture in case the wind gets strong. You know how these storms can cause high winds.'

He looked at his watch.

Nine fifteen.

Other wristwatches were checked up and down the east coast.

In New York City, members of Vinnie Tourino's crime family had been dispatched to a half dozen sites – three jewelry stores, a check-cashing establishment, and two small branches of larger banks.

The Baltimore crime syndicate had selected four targets once the electricity went off: two casinos and two high-end jewelry stores known to have millions in uncut diamonds on hand.

The Philadelphia mob had pinpointed two illegal gambling operations run by its rival gang, two fancy restaurants, a high-end jewelry store, and two suburban bank branches.

The major crime families in these cities, and others, had 'sub-licensed' knowledge of the time the blackout would occur to various lesser gangs in order to recoup their investments.

In Manhattan, the man called Tengku also kept an eye on the time. Four of his followers had positioned themselves along the route that Senator Quinlin would take on his way from the ballroom to his waiting car outside the hotel. As a leading candidate, he would be flanked by Secret Service agents assigned to keep him safe, but Tengku was convinced that the sudden blackout would cause enough confusion to allow his men to overpower the agents and kill Quinlin. If they died in the attempt, so be it. They would be giving their lives for a greater good. All those virgins.

Back in Toronto, Dominick Martone played a video game with one of his grandchildren in the den of his house while his wife, Maria, put the finishing touches on her grandson's favorite dessert, *biscotti dei fantasmi* – 'ghost cookies' – shaped into ghost faces with a cookie cutter and decorated with a sugary icing, chocolate chips the final touch for eyes. She'd already whipped up biscotti with almonds, butterscotch chips, and bourbon for her husband. An orchestral version of *La Boheme* played softly in the background.

Martone, too, checked his watch, but not because he had members of his crime family dispatched in Toronto ready to cash in on the blackout. The Toronto crime boss had already made a large profit on his investment by selling franchises to others, and had no intention of committing criminal acts that night. He left that to the lesser species of crime bosses, the *imbeciles* for whom he had little or no respect.

It was nine thirty up and down the east coast of the United States and Canada.

And then it was nine thirty-one.

TWENTY-SEVEN

'Hey, Paul, you look like hell,' a younger, long-haired co-worker seated next to Saison said as the large French-Canadian stared blankly at the bank of computer screens on which vital data was displayed.

'You don't look so good yourself,' Saison said.

His colleague laughed. 'You been winning at the track lately?'

'*Crétin à crinière,*' Saison muttered, calling him a long-haired twit.

'What's that mean, Paul?'

'You don't want to know. Just shut up, huh. I'm thinking.'

Saison's 'thinking' involved going over and over in his mind what he had to do to initiate the blackout. 'First I do this, then I do that. This must be done before that is done. Seven steps. Do this, then...'

He got up and walked from the room in the direction of the master control room where the switches he was to manipulate were housed. 'First this, then that, then...'

He checked his watch: nine twenty-five.

The control room was vacant. Would he continue to be the only person in the room when the time came to act? He hoped so. He hadn't thought of that until then. His bargain with Smythe didn't call for him to have to become physically violent in order to accomplish his mission. He made a decision: he would not attack anyone. If others came in and thwarted his plan, he would leave, go to Smythe's home anyway, and collect his money.

He looked at his watch: nine thirty-one. He pulled the scrap of paper Smythe had given him with the time and date: Friday, August twenty-second, 2014. Fourteen minutes to go.

His supervisor walked in. Saison shoved the paper back in his pocket.

'Everything OK, Paul?' he asked.

'Yeah, yeah, yeah, everything is A-OK.'

'You pick up any problems on the computers?'

'Nah, no problems. Everything hunky-dory.'

'Well, I saw you in here and—'

'Nothing wrong,' Saison said, realizing he'd begun to sweat. 'Going back now.'

His boss watched him lumber from the control room and thought what he always thought when talking to Paul Saison: *Maybe he'll quit. God, please tell him to quit.*

Saison settled back in his chair in front of

the monitors and looked at the paper again. He checked his watch: nine thirty-one.

Five minutes later, he looked at his watch again: nine thirty-one.

His eyes returned to the computer screens in front of him.

Smythe left the crowd in his living room and found a secluded corner away from the party. He looked at his watch: nine forty-four.

Dominick Martone checked the time: nine forty-four.

Tengku's band of assassins' watches read nine forty-four.

Everyone's watches along the north-eastern coast of North America said nine forty-four.

At Power-Can, Paul Saison's watch still read: nine thirty-one.

TWENTY-EIGHT

A pianist accompanied singers at the Smythe's Steinway grand, including Cynthia, who performed her favorite aria, *Celeste Aida*. It was nine forty-five, and her husband tensed as he waited for the lights to go out and their expensive gasoline generator to kick in.

It didn't happen. He watched the seconds hand slowly sweep across the face of his watch until it read nine forty-six. And nine forty-seven. Nine fifty. Nine fifty-five. Panic set in. Cynthia reached an especially challenging portion of the aria and nailed the high notes, eliciting applause and a few whoops. Smythe felt faint. Why hadn't the lights gone out? What had happened? Why had Saison failed to trip the appropriate switches that would have sent the blackout cascading down the entire north-eastern grid?

'You OK, Carlton?' someone asked, noticing his ashen face. He'd had to lean against a doorjamb to stay on his feet.

'I'm ah ... I ah ... sure, I'm fine.'

He went to the staircase and managed to get to his bedroom where he closed the door and sat on the bed. Who could he call? He pictured Dominick Martone and his goons. Martone would be furious, angry enough to kill. Millions of dollars was resting on the money he'd laid out for the blackout information, millions from other organized crime figures. They, too, would be angry enough to want to kill Martone – and Carlton Smythe.

He took deep breaths to calm himself and decided there was nothing he could do at that moment except return downstairs and act as though nothing was wrong. Whether he could pull that off was pure conjecture.

In Manhattan, presidential frontrunner Senator Miles Quinlin had given a rousing speech to a ballroom filled with well-heeled supporters who'd happily written large checks in return for access to him once he was in the White House. He'd come down from the podium and pressed the flesh, going table to table, flashing his winning smile, saying precisely the right thing in ten words or less to each contributor.

'Time to go, Senator,' an aide whispered in his ear.

'Right. Let's stay on schedule,' Quinlin said, delivering his final words of appreciation to a donor. He followed his aides, and the two Secret Service agents assigned to protect him, from the room.

Although the senator had entered the Hilton through the front door, it had been arranged for him to make his exit through a back corridor used by hotel staff. His car, and two others, waited outside the door to that corridor, engines running, poised to whisk the candidate to his next event.

One of the agents opened the door and stepped out onto the street, immediately followed by Quinlin, two aides, and the second agent. Waiting for them in a knot of a halfdozen onlookers, who'd seen the cars and reasoned that the senator would come through that door, were two armed members of Tengku's small cabal. They'd closely monitored their watches. It was precisely nine forty-five when Quinlin emerged from the hotel. Assuming that the streetlights and twin bulbs above the door would instantly go black, the men, standing close to each other, pulled their handguns from the waistbands of their trousers. But in the illumination from the streetlamps, the agent who'd been first through the door spotted the weapons and threw himself at the would-be assassins, knocking both to the ground. The second agent pushed Quinlin to the pavement where an aide fell on top of him.

One of the assassins' weapons had fallen from his hand and skittered into the gutter.

The other managed to raise his handgun and point it at the second agent who'd also drawn his weapon. The agent squeezed off a shot that hit the armed Tengku cohort between the eyes. As the other would-be terrorist scrambled to his feet, a shot caught him in the stomach. He doubled over and pitched face-first onto the hard sidewalk.

Vinnie Tourino was not a happy man when the lights didn't go out. His crews had been ready to hit their targets the moment it went dark. When it didn't, they abandoned their planned robberies, although one group had been observed hanging around a Tiffany's branch and were picked up by the police.

'That mother-fucking, double-dealing, lying prick Martone,' he snarled. 'I'm gonna personally rip his fucking balls off.'

Alphonse from Baltimore and Tony from Philadelphia also had things to say about Dominick Martone, but weren't as genteel in their choice of words.

Martone also had a generator hooked up to the home's electrical system, and had expected what Smythe had expected, the house to go dark before the generator came online. When it didn't happen, he assumed that his watch might have been running fast and patiently continued playing the video game with his grandson. But after ten minutes he went to his study and called Smythe's home phone number. Mrs Kalich answered, found Smythe, and told him Mr Martone was on the line.

'He called?'

'Yes, sir. He said it was urgent.'

A failed operatic baritone had taken his place alongside the pianist and had launched into a heartfelt version of *Some Enchanted Evening,* made famous in *South Pacific* by Ezio Pinza, as Smythe took the call in his home office.

'What the hell is going on, Smythe?' Martone barked.

'I don't know, Dom, and believe me I'd like to know. I'm really upset and—'

'You lying, conniving bastard,' Martone said. 'When I get through with you you'll be more than upset. You'll be lucky you can even crawl.'

'Please, Dom, I—'

Martone's slamming down of the phone was ear-shattering.

It took until nine fifty-eight for Paul Saison to realize that his vintage watch had stopped. When he finally did, he checked a wall clock, which displayed the correct time. He'd been nipping bourbon from a small silver flask he always carried and was drowsy, having to fight to not doze off in front of the computers he was charged with monitoring.

'*Sacré bleu*,' he muttered as he hauled himself off his chair and headed for the control room. 'Do this, then do this ... first trip the master switch, then the backups ... No, first trip the backup switches and...'

The control room was empty. Saison set about going through the drill he'd been repeating to himself over and over. He looked at the clock: ten twelve. He shook his head to clear the fuzziness from his brain. At ten fourteen, he placed his hand on the master switch and pulled. Ear-piercing sirens went off, and emergency lights came to life. As he started to leave, the shift supervisor and two members of the plant's security team burst into the room.

'What the hell happened?' the supervisor shouted.

Saison shrugged, flung his large hands into the air, and started to walk away.

'You're not going anywhere,' his boss said.

'Hey, why do you say that to me, huh? What do you think, I do something here?'

'Don't let him leave,' the supervisor said as others poured into the room, the warning sirens wailing, multi-colored lights flashing, dozens of voices mingling.

Saison walked to a chair in a corner of the huge room, sat heavily, and lowered his face into his hands.

'You crazy son-of-a-bitch,' Saison's supervisor screamed at him. He turned to the security guards. 'Don't let him leave! Tie the son-of-a-bitch up. Shoot him for all I care.'

Saison looked up and extended his hands in a pleading gesture. He babbled in French, his voice rising and falling, cursing, invoking an unseen god, falling into a sing-song wail, twisting in his chair against the handcuffs that bound his ankles to the chair's legs.

And he cried.

TWENTY-NINE

It was four minutes past ten when the lights went out in Smythe's house, causing surprised shrieks and a few giggles from the guests. Moments later, the generator was automatically activated and a portion of the house's lamps, as well as its refrigeration unit, were given new, low-wattage life.

'How long will the power be off?' people asked those who were wondering the same thing.

Cynthia Smythe instructed Mrs Kalich to bring candles from the pantry to augment the lamps. 'Where is Mr Smythe?' she asked the housekeeper.

'I don't know.'

She forgot about her husband as she busied herself entertaining guests. The pianist began a medley of Broadway show tunes, which prompted singers to join in.

As voices were raised in song, Cynthia's husband was upstairs debating what to do. Martone's anger over the phone was palpable. Would he come to the house looking for him? Smythe pondered. He decided he wouldn't, if only not to embarrass himself in front of Cynthia's friends from the opera company. But he knew that he had to be prepared for whatever did ensue over the course of the night, and the next day, too.

He hurriedly shoved clothing into the carry-on suitcase he used on his trips, and added a few items from his bathroom. Encouraged by the happy sounds of singing – others would be preoccupied – he went down into the kitchen where a single member of the catering staff worked. Smythe placed the carry-on next to the kitchen door and dropped a dish towel over it. He walked into the living room, forced a smile at those who weren't gathered around the piano, and stood by a window overlooking the front grounds and the circular driveway in which a number of cars were parked, effectively blocking access from that direction. His mind raced; bile rose from his stomach and burned his mouth. A vision of Paul Saison in a casket came and went.

'Carlton, come and join in,' Cynthia called from where she stood behind the pianist, hands on his shoulders.

'Oh no,' Smythe said, waving off the suggestion. 'I'm not a singer and...'

His eyes went to the front of the house again. Headlights from two cars played off the others in the driveway. Smythe came closer to the window and narrowed his eyes.

Dominick Martone and four men, including Hugo, got out of the cars and stared at the front door.

An agonized whine came from Smythe as his flight-or-fight instincts kicked into gear. For a moment he considered going to the front door and throwing himself on Martone's mercy: *'It's not my fault, Dom ... That drunken Frenchman Saison fouled up ... You want to kill him, I'll go with you and pull the trigger myself.'*

Instead, he quickly left the living room where the pianist segued from *You Light Up my Life* to *I'm Beginning to See the Light* and went to the kitchen. 'Be right back,' he said to Mrs Kalich as he grabbed the carry-on bag, pulled a set of car keys off a rack, went out the door and ran to where his car and Cynthia's were parked at the rear of the house. He looked down at the keys. He'd taken the ones to her Jaguar instead of his. He got in the Jag, started the engine, and drove slowly up the driveway until reaching where it intersected with the rear street. Everything was dark and quiet. He headed up the road, his eyes as much on his rear-view mirror as on the street in front. He had no idea where to go or what to do. He just knew that he had to get away and find time to think.

He drove with care. There were no traffic lights; a few citizens stood at intersections directing traffic. Without thinking about it, he found himself in the parking lot of the building in which he rented space. Cynthia always kept a flashlight in the glove compartment, and Smythe used it to navigate his way into the building and find his way to his office. He placed the hundred thousand dollars he'd kept there in the suitcase along with various papers he thought he might need. He also decided to take the new laptop he'd purchased and placed that in the suitcase along with the money. As a last thought, he removed a stack of hundred dollar bills and shoved them in his pants and jacket pockets.

What to do next?

He had no idea what was happening with Saison. He'd obviously created the blackout, albeit too late to be effective. Was he now on his way to the pool house to collect the two hundred and fifty thousand dollars in the box with his name on it? The thought of him having that money caused Smythe to growl.

The possibility that Saison had been caught in the process of flipping the switches was chilling. If he had been, he'd be grilled about why he'd done it, and Smythe didn't doubt for a moment that he would tell them that he, Carlton Smythe, had been behind the plan, and *that* would mean that they would be looking for *him*.

The flight he'd booked to Buenos Aires left on Sunday. He'd have to lay low until then.

'No,' he said aloud. If they were looking for him, they'd check all the airports and airlines. He couldn't run the risk. It also dawned on him that if they were seeking him, they'd be canvassing for Cynthia's blue Jaguar.

It was all too much to process at that moment. A wave of exhaustion swept over him. He had to get some rest.

He pulled from the lot and headed for a small motel a few blocks from the office building. He'd noticed it a few times and thought it looked seedy. It wasn't part of a large chain, and he wondered whether it was one of those hot sheets places used by prostitutes.

He pulled up in front and saw that there were lights on, which meant it had an alternative source of power. He grabbed his carry-on and suitcase and entered the front office.

'Good to see that you have power,' he told the older woman behind the desk.

'Generator's working,' she said. 'Not sure for how long.'

'I don't want to continue driving in these conditions,' Smythe said. 'Do you have a room?'

'Yes, I do,' she said and handed him a

254

registration form. 'Credit card?'

'No, no credit card. I'll pay cash.'

Did she view him suspiciously? If so, she didn't say anything to indicate it. He handed over the cash and she gave him a key to a room at the far end of the one-story, ten-room complex.

He drove the car to a secluded spot at the rear of the motel, hoping no one would spot it during the night. He entered the room in which a single table lamp on a small desk provided dim illumination. There was the powerful smell of disinfectant; he'd become sensitive to odors after living with Cynthia's keen nose for so many years. He examined the bedspread, which seemed clean enough, and looked in the bathroom where a leaky faucet had created a rust stain in the sink.

Over the next hour he parted the drapes a dozen times in search of anyone who might be looking for him. Finally he sat at the desk, pulled blank sheets of paper from its drawer, and started to write:

Dear Cynthia,

As I write this, I know how angry you must be and how much you must hate me. I know that I haven't always been the husband you'd like me to be, and I apologize for anything I've done in the past to hurt you. When you get this note I'll be far away and out of your life. While we have had our problems over the years, I don't view our marriage in a negative light. Maybe if we'd had children things might have been different, although I don't think so. Looking to something else, someone else to solve problems never works. The problems were between us, and I'm sorry for those times that I've let you down, as I certainly have now.

I've done a bad thing and hope it won't reflect badly on you. I have to live with it, too. I wish you nothing but good things in your life without me, and would be pleased if you found a great guy and got married again. I'll sign off now.

Love, Carlton

P.S. Sorry I took your car. I didn't hurt it in any way.

He didn't undress for bed. He lay on top of the bedspread and dozed off a few times. Once, the sound of the door being slammed in the next room woke him, and the sounds of a couple having sex penetrated the thin wall. It lasted only fifteen minutes. The door slammed again and a car pulled away.

He thought of Gina.

At six the next morning he left the motel and drove to a small diner. The blackout was still in progress and a large, crude sign in front read: *Gas Grill & Fridge Work-*

ing. Smythe noticed as he pulled behind the building that a Rent-a-Wreck lot was next door. As he paid his bill, he asked the owner what was new with the blackout.

'You'd think those clowns at Power-Can would have it fixed by now,' the owner said.

'Is that where the trouble started?' Smythe asked.

'Yeah. I heard on my battery-powered radio this morning that some crazy Frenchman at the plant deliberately caused it. Seems he wasn't the only one involved.'

'That's really interesting,' Smythe said. 'Did they say who the other people were?'

'Not that I heard. They ought to toss the bastard and whoever else was with him in jail and throw away the key.'

'I agree,' Smythe said, a lump in his throat. 'Thanks for the breakfast. Hope the power comes back on soon.'

He got in the Jaguar, started the engine, and checked the gas. Almost a full tank. He turned on the radio, annoyed with himself that he hadn't thought to do it earlier, and tuned to CFTR-680 News, Toronto's twenty-four-hour news station. After a pod of commercials, the newscaster returned.

'The massive blackout that has crippled all of Eastern Canada and the East Coast of the United States was caused, according to authorities, by the deliberate work of one man, Paul Saison, a French-Canadian engineer at Power-Can where the blackout originated. We've been told by reliable sources that Saison has admitted to having sabotaged the plant, and has named others who were also involved, including a former employee, Carlton Smythe. Smythe's whereabouts are unknown at this point. Stay tuned for further updates on this breaking story.'

Smythe slunk down and emitted a long, slow, painful whine. 'Oh my God,' he said. 'What have I done?'

As he wallowed in self-pity in the luxurious leather seat of the Jag, he looked across the lot at the Rent-a-Wreck one-story building. Its large neon sign had been unlit when he'd arrived. Now, it was glowing. The sign in front of the diner had also come on.

The blackout was over.

Buoyed by that realization – he actually felt proud of those who'd fixed the problem – he got out, took his suitcase with the money and carry-on bag from the trunk, left the key halfway inserted in the ignition, placed the note he'd written to Cynthia on the front seat, and walked to the car rental lot.

'I see that the power is back,' he said to the middle-aged man behind the counter.

'It's about time,' the man said gruffly. 'What can I do for you?'

'I need a car,' Smythe said.

'Not a problem.' He looked at Smythe's luggage and frowned.

Smythe picked up on it. 'I had a taxi drop me at the diner next door,' he said. 'They had the grill working. I thought I'd have breakfast before walking over here to pick up a car.'

The man nodded and pulled out a list of available vehicles. 'Where are you driving to?' he asked.

'Oh, just local. Some business calls I have to make.'

Smythe chose a car.

'Credit card?'

Smythe forced a smile. 'Never use them,' he said, 'but I'll be happy to give you a returnable deposit in cash.'

The man's face mirrored the calculation he was doing. 'Have to be five hundred,' he said, 'plus the daily rental fee.'

'That will be fine,' Smythe said.

'Driver's license?'

Smythe had deliberately not used a credit card for fear that the rental agent had heard news reports on which his name had appeared. But he couldn't refuse to show his driver's license, not to a car rental company. He held his breath as he handed it to the agent – who dutifully noted information from it on the rental form – and exhaled when it was given back to him.

'How long do you want it?' Smythe was

asked.

'Oh, just one day, maybe two.'

Keys in hand, Smythe accompanied the man to a pea green Chevy sedan.

'Nine years old but in tip-top shape. We may rent wrecks but every car has been carefully inspected and serviced.'

'That's good to hear,' Smythe said. 'Thank you.'

He drove to a Starbucks parking lot where he pulled his laptop from the suitcase and went inside. He ordered a latte, found a seat, and turned on the computer, accessed information he needed from the Internet, and sent Gina a short email: *My darling, I am on my way but will be delayed for a week or so, and will be out of touch. Do not worry. I am fine. I love you mi bella amada. I count the minutes until we are together again.*

Afraid that any further emails might be traced, he decided that it would be the last email he would send until reaching South America.

Forty-five minutes later, he left the café, got in the car and drove eighteen miles north in the direction of Buttonville Airport, a small airfield used by charter companies, flight schools, and aircraft rental companies. Before actually entering the airport he found a clothing store in which he purchased a Toronto Blue Jay's baseball cap with a long visor, a sweatshirt, a pair of jeans, sneakers, a tie, and two sets of underwear. Although he'd washed up at the motel before leaving, he felt grubby and in need of fresh clothing and a shower. The gray slacks and blue blazer he'd worn at the party the night before were wrinkled but would have to do a while longer. He put on the tie, checked his hair in the mirror, and pulled into a space reserved for charter passengers at the small airport terminal.

'I was wondering if I could arrange for a flight to Quebec City?' he told the young fellow manning the desk.

'Sure,' was the reply, 'now that the power's back. When do you want to go?'

'The sooner the better,' Smythe said. 'I have a last-minute business deal in Quebec City that I need to close today. It just came up and I can't lose the opportunity.'

'We have a few pilots available.'

'That's wonderful. How long a flight is it?'

'About an hour. Depends on the type of aircraft.'

'The faster the better,' Smythe said.

A half hour later, and after having paid cash – he figured the Rent-a-Wreck owner would eventually find the Chevy and had five hundred dollars for his trouble – he was strapped into the right-hand seat of a sleek twin-engine plane. To his left was the pilot, a solidly-built man with a scraggly red-and-gray beard and a face deeply creased from having peered for too many hours into the sun. They chatted amiably during the hour-long flight.

'Thanks,' Smythe said as he climbed down from the plane at Quebec City's airport and pulled his suitcase and carry-on from where they had been stowed behind his seat.

'No problem,' the pilot said. 'Hope you close that big deal of yours.'

Smythe entered the terminal, plugged in his laptop and read what he'd downloaded onto it while at Starbucks. Satisfied, he re-traced his steps outside and got into a taxi.

'*Où allons nous?*' the driver asked.

'English?'

'Of course.'

'Good. Dalhousie Street please. The port, where the big ships are.'

Quebec City's port is one of the biggest and best in North America. Ships of every size – container ships, tankers, grain haulers, cruise ships – arrive and depart with great frequency. Smythe had accessed information about schedules while at Starbucks and was pleased to see that a tramp steamer, The Bárbara, was scheduled to leave for Brazil the following day.

He'd considered chartering a private jet to Buenos Aires but was afraid that security at the Argentinean airport would be stringent even for a private plane. Besides, it would be too expensive.

He'd finally decided that his best chance to reach South America would be by ship, but not on some fancy cruise. He'd always been fascinated by people who traveled as passengers on cargo ships, and had read a book in which the writer chronicled his adventures sailing the world as one of only a few passengers on a variety of such ocean-going vessels.

As he walked the sprawling port of Quebec City in search of The Bárbara, it soon became evident that lugging the suitcase full of money was too laborious. But what to do with it? He was about to turn around and seek a hotel or motel in which to stash it when he spotted the ship in its berth alongside other, larger vessels. When he got closer he noticed a small, low building with a sign: *Passenger Information*. He went in and approached a table on which a tent card read *The Bárbara*. A pretty, buxom, middle-aged woman with a mane of copper hair and whose black blouse displayed a generous freckled cleavage, sat behind the table reading a magazine.

'Excuse me,' Smythe said. 'Are you selling cabins for passengers on this ship?'

She looked up and gave him a friendly smile. 'That's right,' she said. 'Are you interested in booking passage?'

'As a matter of fact I am,' he replied.

'Has a travel agent arranged it?'

'Travel agent? No, I haven't seen a travel agent. I just...'

She looked at him quizzically, and he knew that she found it strange that a nicely-dressed middle-aged man, sweating profusely and hauling a suitcase with him, would simply show up the day before the scheduled sailing and want to book a cabin.

'I realize that this is last-minute,' Smythe said, 'but I've decided on the spur of the moment to get away.'

'From something?' she asked with a playful smile.

He felt lightheaded and asked if he could take the folding chair next to her.

'Oh, sure,' she said. 'Are you ill?'

'No, no, just tired. You see ... well, I've been going through a very difficult divorce and ... well, I desperately need a change of scene, somewhere relaxing. I've been to South America before on business and loved it there, so I thought by combining a leisurely trip on a cargo ship with some time in a different setting it would help me clear my head and—'

'I understand,' she said. 'Here, have some water.' She handed him an unopened bottle, from which he eagerly drank.

After consulting papers she said, 'We do have an available cabin. It's one of the smaller ones but it's quite comfortable, I assure you. We have a good chef on board, and the other passengers seem like a friendly bunch. Would you be interested in that cabin?'

'Oh yes, I would, very much.'

'Do you have a credit card and identification? And I'll need a passport.'

Smythe said that he would pay in cash.

'That will be fine,' she said, 'but you'll have to include a retainer for miscellaneous charges on board ship, you know, for drinks and other items not included in the fare. By the way, the fare is two hundred dollars a day. That includes three meals of course and, as I said, our chef is terrific.'

'Will five hundred dollars be sufficient for the retainer?' he asked.

She smiled. 'Yes, I think that will be fine.'

He handed her his license and passport and held his breath. While she went to a photocopy machine to make copies, he counted out five hundred dollars, plus enough to cover the fare for fifteen days, which he hoped would suffice.

'Thank you,' he said when she handed him back his passport and license. 'How long will the trip take?'

'It depends upon the weather and sea conditions. No more than fifteen days, probably fewer.'

'That sounds fine.'

He relaxed considerably. 'Is your name Barbara?' he asked.

'No. Why do you ask?'

'The name of the ship. I thought maybe it was named after you.'

Her laugh was earthy. 'No, *bárbara* in Spanish means "great, wonderful".'

'Oh. I didn't know that. Will you be on the ship?'

She nodded as she put together a folder of information for him. 'Everything you need to know is in here,' she said. 'We leave tomorrow afternoon at four. Where will you be staying overnight?'

'I haven't made plans,' he said.

She handed him a card with the name of a motel. 'It's just two blocks from here,' she said. 'Give them this card when you check in. They'll take good care of you.'

He was touched by her generosity of spirit.

'Be back here by one tomorrow. We like to have our passengers on board early.'

'I'm sorry,' he said, 'but if your name isn't Barbara, what is it?'

'Kerry.' She stood and shook his hand. 'See you on board, Mr Smythe. Have a pleasant journey.'

THIRTY

The people gathered in Smythe's living room the following afternoon were not there for a party.

Bill Whitlock, the DEA special investigator, his Canadian counterpart Antoine Arnaud, two Royal Canadian Mounted Police detectives, one from the Criminal Intelligence Program, the other from RCMP's Foreign Drug Cooperation Agency, were joined by detectives from the Toronto Police Service's Organized Crime Enforcement Unit and its Intelligence Services. Private investigator Clarence Miller III had also been invited to attend.

Cynthia Smythe was in a corner of the room on a love-seat, her stockinged feet drawn up beneath her, eyes red from crying, cheeks smeared with mascara that had run. Her mother, Gladys Wiggins, sat staunchly in an antique rocking chair, hands folded primly on her lap, head held high, taking it all in over half-glasses.

'OK, Mrs Smythe, let's go over it again,' the Intelligence Services officer said. 'You had a party here when the blackout occurred. That's when your husband disappeared.'

'That's right.'

'He didn't tell you he was going, didn't say where?'

'No, he just left. He took my car.'

'The blue Jaguar.'

'Yes,' she answered, blowing her nose.

'When did you discover that it was missing?'

'Last night. When I couldn't find him, I went outside. That's when I saw that my car was gone, and then I went into the pool house.'

'And found the box with Mr Saison's name on it and the two hundred and fifty thousand dollars.'

Cynthia gasped, setting off hiccups. 'I was shocked. Where would Carlton have gotten so much money?'

'That's what we're trying to figure out, Mrs Smythe.'

The Organized Crime Enforcement agent entered the conversation. 'You said that Dominick Martone and your husband were in some sort of a business together?'

'Yes.'

'What sort of business?'

'I don't know. Mr Martone – he's a generous man, donates large sums of money to the COC – he and some of his associates

came to the house not long after the blackout occurred.'

'Looking for your husband?'

'Yes.'

'Did he say why?'

'No. He was very polite. When I told him
that Carlton was gone, he and his associates
left.'

'We'll be interviewing Mr Martone later
today.'

One of the Toronto officers' cell phone
rang and he walked from the room. When
he returned he said, 'Your car has been
found, Mrs Smythe.'

'That's wonderful. Where?'

'Behind a diner. The officers who located
it are driving it here now.'

'Was it ... was it damaged?'

'Evidently not. Your husband left a note
for you in it.'

Cynthia got to her feet. 'A note? What did
it say?'

'You'll have to wait until the officers
arrive.'

Whitlock turned to Mrs Wiggins. 'You say
that your son-in-law has a lady friend in
Buenos Aires?'

She referred the question to Miller, who
had remained silent during the questioning.
'Perhaps you should tell him about Carlton's floozy in Argentina,' she said. 'I find it
too distasteful to even discuss.'

Miller explained how Cynthia and her mother had retained him to see whether Mr Smythe was having an affair. 'My man in Buenos Aires confirmed that he was.' He handed photos taken by Popi Domingo to Whitlock, who shared them with the others. 'Her name is Gina Ellanado. Mr Smythe spends intimate time with her whenever he travels to Argentina.'

'He is a liar as well as an adulterer,' Mrs Wiggins said, 'claiming that all his trips to Argentina were for business. The man is a despicable monster.'

Cynthia, who'd resumed her place on the love-seat, said, 'He's gone to Argentina to be with his mistress. I know it, I just know it.'

'He has an airline reservation to Argentina for tomorrow,' Whitlock said, 'but I doubt whether he'll use it. We've contacted all the airlines. If he tries to book passage on any of them we'll know about it. The Toronto PD officers will remain here for the rest of the day and evening in the event he tries to contact you. In the meantime rest assured that we're doing everything possible to locate him. Thank you for your time and co-operation.'

Whitlock and Arnaud had driven together to the house. They pulled from the driveway and went to a fast food restaurant where they ordered coffee and sat in a booth.

'What do you think?' Whitlock asked.

'Hard to make sense of it,' Arnaud said. 'According to this clown Saison, it was Smythe who concocted the scheme to cause the blackout, and that note my future sister-in-law mentioned – the one we took from Saison – nails down when the blackout was supposed to take place. It would have if Saison's watch hadn't stopped. He's admitted that.'

Whitlock sipped and smiled. 'Smythe's wife and mother-in-law seem concerned more about him having a mistress than being behind the blackout. But if Saison is telling the truth – and I have trouble putting much credence in anything he says – Smythe has perpetrated one hell of a scheme.'

'One that generated lots of money for him. You figure Martone is involved?'

'That's my guess, but there's nothing to link him directly. We do know that Smythe flew with Martone to that mob sit-down, and has been spending time with him here in Toronto. We've heard from informants that the mob in New York, Philadelphia, and God knows where else were planning something at the time of the blackout. *And* there was that thwarted attempt on Senator Quinlin's life in New York the night the lights went out. Too much to digest in one sitting. We'll know more when Martone is interviewed.'

'Our people in Buenos Aires are following

up on what's in those packages Smythe sent to his lady friend, Ms Ellanado, by way of Guzman. We have the info from all the shipping firms Smythe used. Anything on his use of his credit cards?'

'Not yet, but I expect something any minute.'

As he said it, his cell phone rang.

'Arnaud here.'

He listened to what the caller had to say. 'Thanks,' he said and ended the call. 'Smythe rented a car from a Rent-a-Wreck outfit,' he told Whitlock, 'and showed his driver's license. The guy at the rental agency recognized the name from news he heard on TV. Let's go.'

An hour later, after taking a statement from the rental agent – and hearing him complain about not knowing where the car he'd rented was, although he failed to mention the five hundred Smythe had given him – they drove to Arnaud's Toronto office.

'Maybe we should give this to Interpol?' Arnaud suggested.

'Yeah, we could, only Smythe hasn't been charged with a crime, at least not yet.'

'Interpol can put out a Blue Notice, name Smythe a person of interest.'

A Blue Notice was a step down from a Red Notice, which was used for individuals who'd been indicted of a crime and were on the lam. The notices go to the 190 countries that comprise the Interpol network.

'Let's do it,' Whitlock said. 'In the meantime I need to talk to Cortez in Buenos Aires.' He laughed.

'What's the joke?' Arnaud asked.

'No joke. I was just thinking about this Argentinean bombshell Smythe has gotten himself involved with. Great-looking lady, at least in the photographs Cortez sent. From everything we know, Smythe has been a model citizen until now. I wonder if he decided to leave his marriage and set up this scheme to get rich because of *her*?'

Arnaud, too, laughed. 'If so, she must be something special. I know this psychiatrist who says that the strength of a single pubic hair is stronger than ten thousand mules.'

'Doesn't sound like a professional diagnosis.'

'But true enough, I suppose. You can never figure what crazy thing a guy in mid-life crisis will do. Let's go talk to Saison again. I can use another laugh.'

The two detectives from the Toronto Police Service chatted amiably in the Smythe living room while waiting for Carlton Smythe to call or make contact by some other means.

Cynthia Smythe and her mother remained upstairs for most of the day and into the early evening.

'Do we have to do this?' Cynthia asked.

'Yes, we do,' her mother replied.

'But what will we do if we find Carlton in Argentina?'

'Just leave that up to me,' Mrs Wiggins said. 'I'll call the travel agent first thing Monday morning and make all the arrangements.' She smiled sweetly. 'I have never given you bad advice, Cynthia dear, have I?'

'No, Mother, you haven't. But Carlton wrote that lovely note and—'

'You never should have read it,' Mrs Wiggins said sharply. 'A lot of meaningless pap.'

'I wish the police had let me keep it. It was mine, written to me.'

'I'm glad they didn't.'

Cynthia wept.

'Oh, stop it, Cynthia. You're acting like a pathetic teenager. Go dry your eyes and think about what you'll pack.' Her acid tone changed to a sunny one. 'Going to Argentina will be like a vacation, two girls on a holiday. Doesn't that sound nice?'

'Yes, Mother, it does,' she said, dabbing at her eyes with a handkerchief.

'Then it's settled. We are going to Buenos Aires!'

THIRTY-ONE

Kerry had been right when she told Smythe that his cabin aboard The Bárbara would be small. But its dimensions pleased him, providing the first sense of security he'd felt since going down the path of criminality. There was something comforting about the confined space, as though the walls had been constructed around him as a shield against the terrible things he imagined were lurking in the shadows, waiting to condemn him to Hell for what he'd done.

The space consisted of bunk beds, although he would not be sharing the cabin; a tiny desk and wooden chair; a closet just large enough to hold a halfdozen hangers – an orange lifejacket was on its sole shelf; a yellow wicker two-drawer chest; and two lamps, one on the desk, the other over the bed. A single porthole afforded a limited exterior view. The cramped bathroom held the requisite sink, toilet, and a shower stall whose dimensions would allow him to use it provided he contorted himself. Most important to him was that everything was spic-

and-span, including two glasses and a pitcher on the desk.

A folder on the lower bunk contained information about shipboard life, the times meals would be served, safety instructions in the event of an emergency, and a one-page set of suggestions on how passengers were expected to comport themselves. The final line read: 'Although we strive to make our passengers as comfortable as possible, this is a cargo ship, not a cruise liner, and the needs of the crew involving its cargo must always take priority.'

'Fair enough,' Smythe muttered as he went up the short ladder and tested the upper bunk. That would be where he would sleep, he decided. As a child he'd always wanted to sleep in a top bunk.

He got down and tested the door's lock, which worked. He went into the narrow hallway and tried the key. That, too, worked. Satisfied, he unpacked his belongings. After checking into the motel the night before, he'd ventured out to a strip mall and purchased another suitcase, as well as additional clothing from an adjacent shop. He checked the ship's instructions and was pleased that there was a laundry room on board, as well as a passenger lounge where a variety of board games could be found. Maybe not all the comforts of home but certainly without the tension.

The suitcase containing the cash was shoved beneath the lower bunk, and he draped a few pieces of clothing over it. A steward would clean passenger cabins and change linens once a week, which suited Smythe. On the day when the steward arrived, he would find an excuse to hang around to ensure that the cash-laden suitcase wasn't touched.

Aided by a tugboat, The Bárbara departed the Port of Quebec a few minutes after four. Feeling its motion filled Smythe with pleasure, and hope. Of course he would have to figure out how to navigate the authorities once the ship reached Brazil, and would then have to make his way to Argentina. But the days at sea would provide time to formulate plans, hopefully ones that would work.

He was surprised at how pleasantly decorated the dining room was, and how nicely the tables were set. The ship's crew occupied most of the room; the small group of passengers had their own section, although they were invited to mingle with off-duty members of the crew.

His biggest surprise, however, was when he arrived there. Kerry, the lovely woman who'd arranged his passage, was at the door functioning as hostess.

'Hello,' she said. 'Welcome aboard. Did you get settled in your cabin?'

'Yes.'

'It is small as I told you but—'

'Oh, no, I like it very much. It's cozy, everything neat as a pin.'

She smiled broadly. 'I'm glad you like it,' she said. 'Come and meet your fellow-passengers.'

The ship's five other passengers were a lively bunch, with the exception of a man with a perpetual scowl who billed himself as a novelist but who'd never had anything published because of 'those crass publishers who wouldn't know a literary classic from amateur pornography.' (Smythe pledged to avoid him whenever possible). There was also a dour young woman who said she was aboard because it was the cheapest way for her to travel to Brazil where her fiancé had recently relocated because of his job; a heavy-set, jolly older man with a full white beard who told the others that after the death of his wife he'd decided to see the world, and doing it as a passenger on a tramp steamer seemed the most glamorous; and an older couple, both retired teachers.

After dinner, the married couple asked Smythe if he played bridge.

'I used to,' he said, 'but I'm afraid I've forgotten how.'

'We'll teach you,' said the wife. 'You'll pick it up again in no time.'

They were right. Smythe soon found

himself immersed in the game which took place in the passenger lounge, a small but nicely furnished space where Kerry tended bar. The man with the white beard rounded out the foursome. He made frequent trips to the bar between hands, his play becoming more erratic with each drink. That didn't matter to Smythe. He enjoyed the companionship, and was more relaxed than he'd been in days. When asked at dinner why he was traveling by tramp steamer he said simply, 'I've been through a difficult divorce and thought sailing to South America on a ship like this would clear my head.'

The game eventually broke up and Smythe was alone in the room with Kerry, who was busy locking up the bar's bottles and glassware. He was again aware of how attractive she was. The skinny black top she wore exposed plenty of breast, both cleavage and on the sides. There was a sensuous aura about her, earthy; he thought of the actress Colleen Dewhurst. He liked her smile, and her perfume was inviting. He took one of two stools at the bar.

'Would you like a drink before I finish closing up?' she asked.

'No, thank you, I've had enough.' He'd nursed two vodka-and-tonics throughout the evening. 'Can I help you?'

'I'm done,' she said. 'It doesn't take long.'

'Where did you learn to be a bartender?'

'I never did. Serving a few passengers doesn't take much knowledge. Calling it a night?'

'I suppose I should but I'm wide awake, thought I'd take a stroll around the ship.'

'Sounds like a good idea. Mind company?'

'No, I'd like that.'

There wasn't much of a deck to stroll, but being outside in the invigorating night air, a full moon's light flickering off the ocean's swells and whitecaps, was sublimely pleasant. They eventually took a couple of chairs to the edge of the deck and sat, their feet propped up on the railing. She'd slipped out of her sandals; even her red-tipped toes were sexy.

'What is this ship carrying?' Smythe asked, more to make conversation than wanting to know the answer.

'Airplane parts for Embraer.'

'The Brazilian aircraft maker? They make good small passenger planes.'

'I'll take your word for it. I've never flown on one.'

'Is that what this ship usually carries?'

She laughed. 'We never know what we're being asked to transport. It's a spur-of-the-moment kind of thing with a tramp ship. We don't have any regular routes like the big ships do. We got this assignment because Embraer needs the parts, and none of the larger ships sailing out of Quebec were scheduled to leave for Brazil for a week or two.'

'It must be exciting spending your life sailing the world,' he said.

'Exciting? I wouldn't call it that. It's a living.'

There was a lull in the conversation until she asked matter-of-factly, 'You're running away from something, aren't you?'

Her comment took him aback. When he'd regained his composure, he said deliberately lightly, 'I guess we're all running from something. As I told you when I booked passage, the thing that I'm running from is a bad marriage and divorce.'

'What was wrong with your marriage?'

'Oh, I don't know, lots of little things, I guess. Isn't that usually the case?' He laughed. 'I know you'll find this silly but we always fought over how to make martinis. Cynthia – that's my wife – she says I put too much vermouth in them. Stupid thing to argue about.'

'Not stupid to her, I suppose.'

'Have you been married?' he asked, feeling comfortable asking it because she'd raised the topic.

'I am married. Karl – he's the captain of this ship – and I get along just fine,' she said. 'He's easier to get along with these days after his operation.'

'Cancer?'

'Yes. Prostate. They removed it. He's not the animal he used to be.'

'Oh.'

There was silence until she said, 'Tell me about the blackout.'

'Pardon?'

'The big blackout that happened a few days ago.'

He didn't know how to respond, so said nothing for a time. Nor did she. Finally, he asked, 'What do you know about that blackout?'

She sighed and adjusted herself in the chair so that she faced him. 'I know that the police are looking for you, Mr Smythe. I know they say that you caused the blackout and—'

'No, I didn't cause it.'

'Not directly from what I've heard on the news. The man they've arrested is a French-Canadian, so naturally there's been a lot written about him and on TV in Quebec. He claims that the idea was yours. I knew the name was familiar when you first approached me but it took me some time to know why. Carlton Smythe. That's the name.'

Smythe got up. 'You're making a mistake,' he said, unable to control the quaver in his voice. 'I—'

'Mr Smythe, please sit down. I'm not your enemy. You're not the first passenger to travel on this ship because he's wanted by the law.'

Smythe placed his hands on the railing and peered out over the vast Atlantic Ocean. For a moment he considered throwing himself from the ship and ending this saga on his terms. He thought of Gina waiting for him in Buenos Aires.

'Come, sit,' she said.

He did, falling back into the chair like a deflated, flattened balloon. She reached across the narrow gap between them and placed her hand on his arm. 'You don't have to worry about me knowing,' she said. 'I'm not about to turn you in to anyone.'

'I don't understand,' he said.

'Let's just say that I'm sensitive to why people sometimes get in trouble and need to escape. It's happened to me. To Karl, too.'

'Karl?'

'The captain. My husband. We've both had our share of troubles, so we're sympathetic to others who find themselves in a jam. Don't get me wrong, Mr Smythe. May I call you Carlton?'

'May you? Yes, sure.'

'You seem like a nice man who made a mistake and is in trouble for it. I sensed that the minute you showed up. I've developed a pretty good sense of people over the years working on the ship, and I knew I was right about you. Then, when I remembered the name of the man on the TV, I knew. You don't have to worry, Carlton. We're supposed to report the names of every passenger traveling with us to another country, but I didn't report you, or register your passport. I'm sure no one except you, me, and Karl know that you're on The Bárbara.'

'Why did you do that?'

She shrugged and wrapped her arms about herself against a sudden, stiff breeze. 'We've done it before,' she said, 'and we can arrange for you to enter Brazil without the authorities knowing about it. Of course, that takes money. It may sound crude but the authorities we work with expect to be compensated. So do we.'

Strangely, Smythe felt relieved. Had she said that she was doing it out of the goodness of her heart, he would have been skeptical, and pessimistic how it would turn out. But she wanted money, which put it on a pragmatic level. He'd read in thrillers that the only good reason to accept someone who wants to become a spy is money. Alleged love of country, or hatred for a government, doesn't cut it with experienced handlers of turncoats. Only a need for money is an acceptable motivation.

'How much?' he squeezed out.

'I don't think that twenty thousand would be unreasonable considering the situation you're in.'

Smythe was faced with a dilemma. The amount she'd cited was perfectly acceptable. He would have gladly paid twice that amount to clear his way into Brazil. The problem was that if he handed over that much money in cash, she would know that he was traveling with lots of money and might attempt to steal everything he had.

Like so many things that had occurred to him recently, he was left without much of a choice. On the one hand, he was being held up by this lovely woman and her husband for twenty thousand dollars. On the other hand, it was his good fortune to have ended up on a ship with people with larceny in their souls who offered a solution to the huge problem of entering Brazil without having to go through Customs and other stumbling blocks.

Would they deliver on their promise to grease the skids for him to enter Brazil?

Would the rest of his money be safe after he handed over twenty thousand in cash?

'All right,' he said. 'I'll get the money and bring it back to you.'

'You won't be sorry,' she purred.

Ten minutes later he handed over the packets of cash.

'Do you want to count it?' he asked.

'No. I think you're an honorable man who made a mistake. You're not the cheating type.'

With that, she wrapped her arms around him, pressed her ample body against his, and kissed him hard on the mouth.

'Sleep tight,' she said. 'See you at breakfast.'

THIRTY-TWO

Had he not wanted desperately to reunite with Gina, Smythe would have been content to spend the rest of his life on The Bárbara. The ship had a shelf of dog-eared paperback novels, and he whiled away his days at sea reading, napping, eating, playing bridge, and breathing in the salty ocean air. It was idyllic, and he discovered an inner peace that had long been absent.

He was introduced to Karl, the ship's captain and Kerry's husband, and spent time on the bridge, as did the other passengers. Karl was a beefy Brazilian of few words and a gruff demeanor, although he was not unpleasant. A jagged scar across his forehead and a cocked eye testified to his life not having been without incident. The only conversation of substance Smythe had with him was on the last day at sea.

'Kerry will take care of everything,' he said. 'You talk to her and you do what she tells you to do. Once you are in Rio you're on your own. Our job, it is finished. Understand?'

'Yes,' Smythe said, 'and I want to thank you for being ... well, for being understanding and for helping me.'

'Why not?' Karl said. 'Good luck.'

Kerry's kiss the night he'd delivered the money to her had lingered on Smythe's lips and in his memory for the duration of the journey. He had the feeling that if he pursued it she might be willing to go to bed with him, and the contemplation was appealing if not ego-building. But he fought the urge. He was not about to run foul of her husband. More importantly, he would not be unfaithful to Gina.

And so as the trip approached its end, he read books and sat in the sun and dreamed of what life would be like with Gina in their lovely little cottage, the two of them, madly in love and united against the world.

As The Bárbara transported Carlton Smythe to Rio de Janeiro, Paul Saison looked out the window of his Toronto hospital room and did what he'd been doing ever since being transferred there from his jail cell after complaining of chest pains. He cursed Smythe over and over – *'Imbécile!'* *'Tête d'epingle!'* *'Balourd!'* *'Bandit!'* *'Cinglé!'* *'Arriéré!'* – in between bouts of crying.

'Maybe we should increase his medication?' one of the psychiatrists said to a colleague when discussing Saison's condition. They'd been brought onto his case by the cardiologist who'd become concerned about his patient's mental state. When Saison was granted one call to Angelique, she told him to drop dead, which resulted in a tirade about women that generated blushes from the nurses and necessitated his being restrained.

'Probably,' the second psychiatrist concurred. 'The prosecutor in his case isn't happy. The lawyer assigned to defend him is claiming that he's mentally deficient and isn't fit to stand trial.'

'Not our problem. Let's increase the dosage and see if it does any good.'

It didn't.

Dominick Martone could have used a cardiologist the night things went awry at Power-Can. He was livid, and the irate calls from the other Mafia leaders up and down the East Coast didn't help. Had Smythe been home when Martone and his 'associates' arrived that night, the police might have been investigating a murder instead of a blackout.

But by the time the police interrogated the Toronto crime boss, he'd calmed considerably. He'd worked out a repayment of the franchise fees he'd been paid, and an uneasy peace had been reestablished between the families.

'Look, Mr Martone, we're not accusing

you of anything, but we do know that you and Mr Smythe had been spending time together,' one of the two detectives said. 'Smythe's wife says that you were involved in some sort of business deal.'

'We discussed it,' Martone said, nonchalantly draping an arm over the chair. 'It didn't work out.'

'What sort of business was it?'

Martone glanced at the two lawyers who'd accompanied him to headquarters before answering. 'Smythe's an engineer, you know, a slide-rule kind of guy, numbers and figures and things like that. He wanted me to hire him for one of my enterprises but he didn't have anything that I needed.' He came forward and adopted a sincere expression. 'I can't believe the guy would pull a stunt like this, paying some bum inside the plant to pull the switch on the electricity. Good thing I have a generator. You have a generator?'

'No, I don't, Mr Martone. You and Mr Smythe flew to outside Philadelphia where a gang war broke out. People were killed. Do you—?'

'Wait a minute, Detective,' Martone said, holding up his hand. 'Gang war? There was no gang war. I was there having a meeting with business associates and some punks decided to shoot up the place. I had Smythe with me because I thought that maybe if things worked out at the meeting he'd have a job. I was doing the guy a favor. His wife, a terrific woman, is on the board of the Canada Opera Company. You ever go to the opera?'

'No.'

'Any time you want to go, just let me know. I'm a big supporter of COC. I'll comp you.'

The interview ended as the detectives assumed it would. Dominick Martone was untouchable in Toronto, and had his bases covered. One of the detectives told his partner after they'd left that his wife had always wanted to go to the opera. 'Maybe I'll take the old guinea up on his offer.'

In Buenos Aires, the team headed by Luis Cortez had intercepted the packages containing cash that Smythe had sent to Guillermo Guzman. When they discovered that the packages contained large amounts of money, Bill Whitlock in Washington ordered them to record the amount of cash in each package, carefully reseal them, and allow the delivery to go through with the goal of identifying those to whom Guzman distributed the funds.

Gina Ellanado hadn't heard from Smythe since the email he'd sent before fleeing Toronto. Had she been a woman who was interested in world news she might have heard reports about the blackout and the ongoing investigation into whether one Carlton Smythe had been involved. But her TV watching habits included soap operas and old movies, and she seldom read a newspaper. The news depressed her and so she avoided it.

She'd spent most of her time at the cottage she'd rented with the money Smythe had given her, adding decorative touches, stocking the bar with expensive liquors, and bringing what she termed a *'femenino tacto'* to the surroundings. She bought luxurious bedding, colorful tapestries to hang on the walls, and a compact CD player on which she played tango music.

She called Guzman repeatedly to see whether the money had arrived, to be told that it hadn't but that it should be there any day. On this day when she called, he had good news. 'The money is here, Gina. I'm taking my commission and depositing it in my private bank. No sense losing interest while we wait for your friend Mr Smythe to arrive.'

'Yes,' she said, 'that would be good.'

Guzman hung up and looked at Luis Cortez and two plainclothes officers from the Buenos Aires Provincial Police who sat across his desk from him.

'Satisfied?' he said.

'You did good, Guillermo.'

Guzman sneered. 'The money's a private investment from a client of mine. You've got no right coming in here and threatening me. It's a legitimate transaction.'

'Not if it's money gained through a criminal act,' Cortez said.

'Who says it is?' Guzman asked defiantly.

'*We* do,' Cortez replied. 'We'll keep the money safe until our investigation is over. In the meantime stay away from Señorita Ellanado. If she calls again tell her the money is invested and waiting for Smythe to arrive. And keep your mouth shut. We don't have to take you in to be sure you don't talk about this, do we?'

'Take me in for what?'

Cortez shrugged. 'Money laundering, running a criminal enterprise, maybe fraudery.'

'Fraudery? What the hell is that?'

'What we'll accuse you of. Have a good day, and thanks for your cooperation.'

In a suite at the Alvear Palace in Buenos Aires, arguably the city's most expensive hotel – with Cartier across the street and Hermes next door – Cynthia Smythe and her mother, Gladys Wiggins, sat in the living room while the personal butler provided to every guest room meticulously unpacked their luggage in the master bedroom. They'd just arrived and were weary from the trip.

'What do we do first?' Cynthia asked.

'First we nap, dear. Then we have an appointment with Mr Miller's colleague here, Mr Domingo. We'll decide what to do after that, depending upon what he tells us.'

'I—' Cynthia welled up.

'What's the matter, dear?'

'I'm afraid to confront Carlton.'

'Nonsense.'

'I—'

'Go on, say what's on your mind. Don't snivel.'

'I know that he's cheated on me, and that he's a wanted man because they think he was behind the blackout, but he's been a good husband in so many ways that—'

'He's a scoundrel!'

'But after you caught Daddy cheating you stayed married to him.'

'A pragmatic decision.'

'What if Carlton sees how wrong he's been and begs me to stay with him?'

'I seriously doubt that will happen, Cynthia, but we shall see. In the meantime let's nap and browse Cartier before seeing Mr Domingo. It's so convenient.'

THIRTY-THREE

Smythe, his suitcases and carry-on at his side, watched from the deck as The Bárbara entered Rio's Guanabara Bay and approached one of the Port of Rio's multiple wharfs at the foot of the downtown area. As it nuzzled up to the Gamboa Wharf and lines were secured, he was consumed with parallel, conflicting feelings.

Until that point and for the past fifteen days his life had been easy; he hated to see it end. At the same time a sense of anticipatory joy overtook him. He was on the final leg of this unlikely journey, and he wondered how he'd managed to survive the ordeal.

Kerry had instructed him to have his luggage with him on deck and to not join the other passengers when they disembarked and went through Customs and other document verification stations. He was to wait until she personally escorted him from the ship.

After an hour had passed he began to wonder whether she would show up. She did fifteen minutes later. 'Come,' she said. 'Say nothing. Just follow me.'

She led him to an older uniformed government inspector who stood far removed from the main area through which passengers passed. She handed the man an envelope. He grunted, slipped it into his pocket, and nodded. Kerry and Smythe passed his checkpoint and came around the side of a warehouse.

'Welcome to Rio,' she said, smiling.

'That's it?' he said.

'Did you expect a samba band to welcome you? You're safely in Brazil now. I wish you nothing but the best.'

'I don't know how to thank you,' he said.

'No need to,' she replied. With that she wrapped her arms about him and kissed him as she had fifteen nights ago, on the lips, firmly, longer this time.

'You're very sexy,' he said when they'd disengaged.

'Thank you. You're kind of cute yourself. Go now, and good luck.'

He lugged his luggage past a succession of warehouses until he emerged from the pier into streets that led to the city's thriving downtown. He found a *botequin*, a coffee café, with a few outdoor tables. He took one, but an employee told him to buy a chit from the cashier and take it inside where he would be served his *cafezinho*, a tiny cup of strong, black coffee. Smythe had the counterman add milk, before taking his drink back outside where he sipped, watched the parade of well-dressed people, and thought.

He knew that the completion of his trek was near, but it seemed impossibly distant at that moment. Despite the help he'd received from Kerry and her husband, his sense was that the sooner he left Brazil the better. His obvious move would have been to catch a flight to Buenos Aires, but he was still reluctant to chance going through airport security. From what research he'd done, he decided that his best bet was to take a bus, a forty-five-hour trip. The thought of sitting on a bus for that length of time was anathema to him, but there didn't seem to be a sensible alternative.

As he finished his coffee, a boy selling newspapers, both Brazilian and English language editions, hawked his wares to customers in the outdoor café. Smythe motioned for him and took the paper that was in English, handing the newsboy a ten dollar bill. 'Keep the change,' he said. *'Por usted.'* The boy thanked him profusely before continuing down the street.

Smythe took the paper with him to read on the trip. He asked a woman for directions to the bus station and she directed him to the Novo Rio Bus Station on Avenue

Francisco Bicalho, adding that it was only a short walk.

He reached the terminal and went to a ticket window where he was told that there was a bus leaving for Buenos Aires in four hours.

'Is it really a forty-five hour trip?' Smythe asked.

'*Si, señor.*'

'How can the driver drive that long?'

The clerk, who spoke good English – everyone in Rio seemed to – smiled and said, 'We have two drivers on the bus, and a small place for them to sleep. But I make a suggestion to you.'

'Yes?'

'Many people who take this trip go only halfway on the first day. They spend the night in a hotel at Foz de Igauzu, a very beautiful place with a waterfall so big it is three times larger than the Niagara Falls. If you like, I can make a reservation for you at the Hotel das Catartas, a very nice hotel, good restaurants, beautiful scenery. If you do this, there will be a bus in the morning that will take you for the rest of your journey to Buenos Aires.'

Smythe thought for a moment. The contemplation of spending forty-five consecutive hours on a bus was painful.

'Yes, I would like to do that,' he said.

With ticket in hand and a slip confirming

his hotel reservation, he stopped in a book-store and bought two murder mysteries from the English language section, then found another sidewalk café where he told the beautiful waitress – every woman in Rio was beautiful, he decided, each a model for the song 'The Girl From Ipanema' – that he wanted to drink and eat things that were typically Brazilian. She recommended the country's national cocktail, *caipirinha*, made with sugar cane rum, sugar and lime juice, and a shrimp dish, *vatapa*, served with cashew peanut sauce. He ordered both, and by the time he was due to board the bus he'd consumed three of the drinks and was tipsy.

It was a double-decker bus, sleek and shiny, with a toilet area, a mini-bar and snack kiosk, and wide, comfortable, reclin-ing seats, which made napping easy. He'd purchased a *leito* ticket, First Class, and was impressed with the amenities. With the buzz from the drinks numbing his senses, he happily settled into his assigned seat, stretched and yawned, and promptly dozed off.

He awoke an hour later and started read-ing one of the novels he'd purchased. He soon lost interest in the story and pulled the newspaper from his carry-on. The first four pages contained news of goings-on in Rio de Janeiro and the nation of Brazil. Pages five and six provided a recap of news from around the world. The item from Toronto, Canada, immediately grabbed his attention.

The headline read: *Blackout Culprit Dies.*

Ontario, Canada. The French-Canadian man suspected of causing the massive blackout that paralyzed the east coast of the United States and Canada, Paul Saison, an employee of Power-Can where his alleged sabotage took place, has died. The cause was heart failure. Mr Saison had implicated a former employee of the plant, Toronto citizen Carlton Smythe, who is currently being sought by authorities.

But the senior prosecutor assigned to the Smythe case stated in a press conference that because of Mr Saison's mental incapacity following his arrest and prior to his death – he was the only witness against Mr Smythe – the government has decided to drop charges against Mr Smythe, whose whereabouts is still unknown.

A moment of sincere sadness at hearing that the big, bumbling, obnoxious Saison had died was soon replaced by elation. Could it be true? It had to be. He, Smythe, was no longer a suspect? Charges had been dropped?

He let out a yelp that caused others to turn to him.

'Sorry,' Smythe said. 'I've just had good news.'

He read the article multiple times, searching for a word or phrase that would temper his joy. He didn't find one. He wondered about the transporting of large sums of money out of the US to another country, falsely claiming the packages contained books. Had that broken the law? Probably. But it was a minor concern compared to having been fingered as the brains behind the blackout. At least that was the way he processed it as the bus roared down the highway taking him to Buenos Aires – to Gina.

He was in an expansive mood as he stepped off the bus in Foz de Igauzu and checked in to the hotel. His room was handsomely decorated and comfortably appointed. He stepped out on to the balcony and was awed by the majesty of the falls. Despite the twenty-hour bus ride, he felt invigorated and energized. 'Life is good,' he said aloud a number of times as he prepared to go downstairs for a drink and dinner, and that upbeat mood didn't abate even after so many *caipirinhas* that he lost count. Before going to bed he decided to break his silence on the Internet and emailed Gina, saying that they would be together again in a few days, together forever. *'When I come to the door of our love cottage, my darling, it will be the first day of the rest of our lives. I will make us martinis and we will toast our good fortune. Yours forever, Carlton.'*

301

The first half of the trip had gone by quickly. Now, in the home stretch, each minute seemed an eternity, and he wanted to go to the driver and urge him to drive faster. Eventually the bus pulled into the huge central bus station in the heart of downtown Buenos Aires. Smythe collected his two large suitcases from where they had been stowed in a compartment beneath the bus and made his way toward the exit. But he had to go to the bathroom and went into a men's room. He looked at himself in the mirrors above the sinks and didn't like what he saw. He was disheveled and weary, his clothing wrinkled, his face sallow and with a day's growth of gray beard. He couldn't arrive at the cottage in that state, and made a decision on the spot to delay seeing Gina until he presented the right image.

'The Four Seasons hotel,' he told the taxi driver.

The suite in which he usually stayed was available. After a shower and shave, he consulted the concierge: 'Where is the best men's clothing store?'

The concierge recommended two, Sir Greyton for the best dress shirts, and James Smart for suits. Smythe liked their British-sounding names and headed for Sir Greyton with a spring in his step. After purchasing two of the shop's most expensive shirts and three silk ties, he went to James Smart where he told the proprietor that he needed the best suit in the shop, and had to have it expertly tailored by the end of the day. The proprietor said that would be impossible, but when Smythe said he would pay double the suit's cost, a tailor suddenly appeared from the back of the shop and Smythe was fitted.

'You will have your suit in an hour,' the proprietor said.

At six, Smythe picked up the suit and returned to the hotel where he tried it on, and selected a shirt and tie to go with. He checked his email. There was nothing from Gina, which didn't concern him. He debated going to the cottage but thought better of it. It was evening. Best to wait until the following day when he would be rested and ready for love. He emailed her that he would be arriving at the cottage the next day and asked that she wait there for him, saying that he wasn't sure what time he would arrive.

He relived that fateful evening when they'd first met by going to the Le Dime bar and having a glass of *cerveza*, the same brand she'd drank, and a bottle of Malbec. For dinner in Le Mistral he ordered the same dish he'd enjoyed that first night, a New York strip steak with the thick herb sauce, *chimichurri*. The harpist's lovely melodies completed the reenactment.

He went to his suite, sated, tired, and

supremely happy. He would have a full night's rest before dressing in his new clothes and arriving at the cottage.

He hadn't realized how tired he'd been and was surprised when he slept until nine the following morning. After a shower and multiple checks of his appearance in the mirror, he descended to the lobby carrying only the suitcase containing the cash. The doorman hailed a cab for him.

'Before we go to my destination,' Smythe told the driver, 'I must stop at a florist, a very good one.'

Ten minutes later Smythe emerged from a shop carrying two dozen red roses. He got back in the cab and gave the driver the address of the cottage.

'That is a long trip,' the driver said.

'It doesn't matter how much it costs,' Smythe said. 'Here.' He handed a hundred dollar bill over the driver's seatback. 'And if the meter says it is more I will pay it, and add a generous tip.'

The ride took a half hour. During it, Smythe silently rehearsed what he would say when Gina opened the door. He had a whimsical vision of her being naked when she did, which brought a wide smile to his face.

'Life is good!' he said aloud, causing the driver to turn his head.

'I am a happy man,' Smythe explained.

The driver laughed. 'Good for you, amigo,' he said.

They pulled up in front of the cottage and Smythe immediately spotted a car parked off to the side. He'd encouraged Gina to rent a car and was glad that she had. With a final payment to the driver including the large tip he'd promised, Smythe watched the taxi drive off. It was a sunny day, the breeze gentle and refreshing. He drew a deep breath, squared his shoulders, and approached the front door. Should he knock or simply walk in? He decided to knock. He cocked his head as he heard the rustle of someone approaching the door.

He pulled himself to his full height, held the roses perfectly upright in an offering position, and was poised to mouth the words that he'd been practicing.

The door opened.

'My darling, I am—'

He was immobilized, in shock and speechless. The roses slipped through his hands and fell to the ground.

'Cynthia?'

'Hello, Carlton,' his wife said. 'We've been expecting you.'

He looked beyond her to where Mrs Wiggins sat facing the door, half-glasses low on her nose, a knowing smile on her face. The joyous, happy music of Donizetti's *La Fille du Régiment* filled the air.

305

He tried to say something but words wouldn't come.

'Come in, Carlton,' Cynthia said. 'Don't just stand there. Are the roses for me?'

'What?'

'The roses. They're beautiful. You'd better pick them up before you step on them.'

She stepped aside to allow him to enter.

'Hello ... Mom,' he managed.

'Hello, Carlton.'

'I ... ah—'

'Do you like what we've done with this charming cottage?' his mother-in-law asked. 'Of course we've only had a few days since buying it but I think we've managed quite nicely, don't you?'

'You ... you've bought this cottage?'

'And at a very reasonable price,' the older woman said. 'You might say it was a steal. Of course, Walter taught me well how to make prudent use of money.'

'Where is—?'

'Your friend, Ms Ellanado? She's gone. She was quite reasonable, too. It didn't cost much to send her on her way, especially when it was pointed out that you are a hunted man, and that being with you would be bad for her. She sold herself quite cheaply, Carlton, but then again that sort usually does.'

He laid the roses on a table and fell into a chair, shaking his head and mumbling something unintelligible.

'Like my new dress?' Cynthia asked, posing in front of him. 'Mother and I have had a wonderful shopping experience in this lovely city.'

'You sent Gina away?'

'Yes.'

'And you bought this cottage?'

'Yes. When we discovered it, Mother convinced me that it would make the perfect winter getaway for us. You know how cold the winters have been recently in Toronto.'

Smythe stood and took steps in the direction of the door.

'No need for you to go, Carlton,' Cynthia said. 'When I first learned that you had this woman here in Argentina I was devastated, as you can imagine. But time heals all wounds. Doesn't it, Mother?'

Mrs Wiggins answered with a smile and raised eyebrows.

'So no need for you to go, Carlton,' Cynthia repeated. 'I've forgiven you, although I'm sure you'll understand that it will take some time for trust to be restored between us. But in the meantime we might as well celebrate being together again. There's a nicely stocked bar in the back. Why don't you make us martinis? And Carlton, p-l-e-a-s-e, not too much vermouth.'

THIRTY-FOUR

And so Carlton Smythe, fifty-one-year-old mild-mannered electrical engineer and long-suffering husband, had returned home. He'd come full-circle since concocting the plan that would free him to pursue the voluptuous Gina Ellanado and live a life of luxury with her in their love-cottage on a hill in Argentina. He'd failed.

He, his wife Cynthia, and his mother-in-law Gladys Wiggins, spent the week in the Buenos Aires cottage before returning to Canada. The women commandeered the cottage's only two bedrooms; Smythe slept on the couch, which was where he preferred to be. Mother and daughter went on a daily shopping spree, insisting on modeling their new wardrobes for him. 'Nice,' was all he could manage to say. 'Very nice.'

His only foray from the cottage was to meet with Argentinean authorities about the money they'd confiscated from Guillermo Guzman, the 'private banker' who'd once been Gina's lover and to whom Smythe had sent the bulk of the cash he'd been paid by

Dominick Martone. There was talk of charging Smythe with money laundering, but it was ultimately decided that it wasn't worth the expense or the time to put him through the legal wringer. As one of the detectives commented during these discussions, 'Let the *ignorante* go. He's pathetic.' The decision was helped along by Mrs Wiggins' pledge of ten thousand dollars for an Argentinean poor children's aid program, the check made out personally to the lead detective. Business as usual.

With two steamer trunks loaded with the clothing the women had purchased in Buenos Aires' most expensive shops, the trio flew back to Toronto. Smythe, of course, was questioned by the Canadian authorities about his possible involvement in the blackout that had inconvenienced millions of people up and down the eastern coast of the United States and Canada. The family attorney coached him on how to answer their questions, and he denied any wrongdoing, pointing to Paul Saison as a demented man whose accusations prior to his *timely* death were the babblings of a madman.

'What about the money in the box in your pool house?' Smythe was asked.

'I have no idea where that came from,' he replied. 'Saison must have stashed it there in anticipation of causing the blackout. Where he got it is beyond me.'

Smythe never did know where the two hundred and fifty thousand dollars he'd left for Saison ended up. The authorities said they would keep it as evidence. Evidence of what? It didn't matter. What was important to Smythe was that he was off the hook. With no concrete evidence on which to base a case – and because the Argentinean authorities declined to become involved – the matter was dropped, to everyone's profound relief. The Wiggins family heritage and reputation had been spared.

Smythe was surprised that he was able to lie with such aplomb. If nothing else his adventure had instilled in him a cunning that had not existed prior to his journey.

Two weeks after their return, the Canadian Opera Company premiered Mozart's opera *Cosi Fan Tutte*, whose translation is 'Thus do all women', or as some phrase it, 'Women are like that'. Smythe tried to weasel out of going, but Cynthia insisted. Although neither she nor her mother had brought up Smythe's ill-fated, harebrained scheme since returning from Buenos Aires, the unstated rule in the household was clear: from now on you do what you're told – or else! Smythe had read Jean Paul Sartre's *No Exit* in which Sartre observed that Hell was spending the rest of your life with people you hated. The man knew what he was talking about.

Smythe had had no communication with Dominick Martone, and hoped that he never would. And so he accompanied Cynthia to opening night with grave trepidation, dreading that the Mafia boss would be there. His worst fears were realized when, as he walked into the vast lobby with Cynthia on one arm and Mrs Wiggins on the other, he saw Martone and his wife Maria chatting with other opera-goers. He looked for Hugo and his ferret-faced colleague but they were nowhere to be seen.

'Excuse me,' Smythe told Cynthia and her mother, 'I have to use the bathroom.' He was on his way to the restrooms when Martone's voice stopped him. 'Hey, Smythe.' Martone broke away from the others and headed in Smythe's direction.

Smythe braced himself for the verbal onslaught – and maybe an onslaught of a more physical variety – as Martone closed the gap, smiled, extended his hand and said, 'Good to see you, pal.'

'I, ah ... yes, it's good to see you, too, Mr Martone. Ah, Dominick. Dom.'

'How've you been?'

'OK, I guess. I—'

'Relax. You look like a deer caught in the headlights. Come on, I want to talk to you.' He grabbed Smythe's elbow and ushered him across the lobby and out the door to the plaza in front of the theater.

'I just want you to know, Dom, that—'

Martone waved his index finger in Smythe's face. 'I talk, you listen. *Capisce?*'

Smythe nodded.

'I got to admit that when this thing of yours didn't go down, I was mad, pretty damn mad. I had some business colleagues who were out to string me up.'

'I know that and—'

Another finger in Smythe's face. He glanced at Martone's other hand to see if it held a gun and was relieved that it didn't.

'I'll level with you, Smythe. I thought about killing you.'

Thought about it? Past tense?

'But then I got to thinking, here I was being taken in by a pretty smooth operator for a million two-fifty. That's not me, Smythe. Nobody puts anything over on Dominick Martone – nobody! So I thought to myself, maybe it's time to take it as a signal, pack it in, get out while I can.' He pulled two cigars from his jacket and handed one to Smythe.

'I thought you quit smoking?' Smythe said.

'I did.' He extended a lighter and lit both cigars. 'I said to Maria, what am I trying to do, live to be a hundred? What am I busting my hump every day for, to make money for other people? Hell, I've got all the money I could ever spend. I'm rich as Croesus. You know him?'

'Some character from Shakespeare?'

Martone slapped him on the back. 'He was a king back before even Christ was born. Rich as...' Another slap on the back. 'Rich as Dominick Martone.' He laughed as he exhaled, sending a cloud of smoke into Smythe's face. 'So I figured that maybe I'm losing it, you know, not as sharp as I used to be. And in my business, Smythe, that can get a man killed.'

Smythe had relaxed considerably since exiting the theater. He drew on his cigar and sent a perfect smoke ring into the air. Martone seemed content to simply smoke and not say anything else.

'What about all the people you sold franchises to?' Smythe asked, filling the void.

'Those buffoons? That's what they are, Smythe, buffoons, without half a brain between them. I paid 'em back, every cent.'

'That's good to hear,' Smythe said, 'I know that I cost you a lot of money, Dom.'

'Yeah, you did, a million two-fifty, but easy come, easy go. That's chump change to me. You know, Smythe, I got to hand it to you. You put one over on this ageing goomba, and you know what?'

'What?'

'You taught me a lesson, woke me up, told me it was time to quit, sit back, smell the roses – and the cigars. You like that cigar? Cuban. You can't buy 'em in the States 'cause the Americans think they'll run Castro out 'a Cuba by not letting Americans buy his cigars. Pretty stupid, huh?'

'I guess it is, Dom.'

'So you don't have to worry about me getting revenge on you for what you did to me. You think I'd hurt somebody who's married to a wife like yours? Your wife's a saint, Smythe, one-of-a-kind, and her mother is a winner, too. You're a lucky man.'

Smythe didn't know what to make of Martone's unsolicited praise of Cynthia and her mother, but he wasn't about to probe. What mattered was that he wouldn't be killed and fed to the fishes.

'Good cigar,' he told Martone. 'Thanks.'

A bell sounded, informing theater-goers that the performance was about to begin. Martone and Smythe extinguished their cigars and returned to the lobby where Cynthia and her mother were talking with Maria Martone. They took their seats in a special section reserved for board members and prime donors to the opera company. The Martones sat directly in front of Smythe and his wife and mother-in-law. The lights dimmed, the orchestra launched into the overture, and Mozart's *Cosi Fan Tutte*, the semi-tragic comic opera, one of the last Mozart had written, came to life on the stage, the singers' powerful voices filling the large hall and eliciting bursts of applause, and cries of 'Bravo' following particularly moving arias.

The production received a standing ovation – every production had the audience on its feet, it seemed to Smythe – and he enthusiastically joined them. But as the applause waned, the president of COC's board stepped through the curtains and came to a microphone that had been carried center-stage by a stagehand.

'Ladies and gentlemen, may I please have your attention,' the president said. 'And will Cynthia Smythe join me here on the stage.'

Smythe looked at his wife, who patted his hand, left her seat, and carried a beaming smile to the stage.

'What's going on?' Smythe asked Mrs Wiggins.

'Quiet,' she commanded.

'We have a very special announcement to make this evening,' said the president, 'but I think it would be more appropriate for Mrs Smythe to tell you about it.'

Cynthia stepped to the mike, cleared her throat, and said, 'Would Mr Dominick Martone please join us.'

Martone got up, turned, waved to the crowd, and took his place alongside Cynthia and the president.

Cynthia kissed him on the cheek and said

into the microphone, 'This is a very special occasion we're celebrating tonight. As many of you know, Dominick Martone has been the most generous supporter of the company for many years. Your board-of-directors felt it only fitting that his love of opera, and financial backing of every production, be honored.'

With that, a giant screen was lowered and a picture of an artist's rendering of a large statue of none other than Dominick Martone was projected on it. The audience burst into sustained applause and continued until the president asked for quiet. 'It is through the generosity of Mr and Mrs Martone, and a sizeable contribution from the Smythe family, that this much-deserved tribute is about to become a reality. In honor of Mr Martone, the plaza will be named Martone Piazza, and this larger-than-life statue will be erected at its center. If all goes to schedule, the unveiling should take place six months from now.'

There was more applause. Tears ran down Martone's cheeks as he embraced Cynthia, extended both hands to the audience, and repeated over and over, *'Grazie! Grazie!'* His wife turned and hugged Mrs Wiggins and Smythe. Martone and Cynthia rejoined them and there were hugs all around. As the Martones and Smythes went up the aisle toward the lobby, Martone whispered in

Smythe's ear, 'See why I let you off the hook, pal? It was your lucky day that you married her. Otherwise...'

A party in the lobby to celebrate the announcement of the Martone statue lasted into the wee hours. Once home, Cynthia insisted that they have a nightcap before going to bed. She was already somewhat tipsy, and giddy with the way the evening had gone. Smythe poured them snifters of Cognac and they settled in the living room. Cynthia raised her glass and said, 'To opera!'

'That was quite a surprise,' Smythe said, understating what he was actually thinking.

'We have another surprise for you,' Cynthia said.

'Oh?'

'I have contractors coming tomorrow to give us an estimate on enlarging the pool house into an apartment for mother.'

'That's ... ah ... that sounds like a good idea,' he managed.

Gladys Wiggins looked at him over her half-glasses and smiled frostily.

Mrs Wiggins excused herself and went off to bed in the guestroom. Cynthia moved closer to Smythe on the couch and said, 'I want you to know, Carlton, that I forgive you. I was so angry, but Mother – she's so wise – assured me that you had suffered what many men suffer, a mid-life crisis.'

'Is that what it was?'

'Of course, darling.'

She put her snifter down on the coffee table, giggled, and kissed his ear. 'Want to cuddle tonight?' she asked in the little girl's voice that she used on occasion, and snuggled up against him.

Smythe sat rigidly, his face void of emotion, staring straight ahead. Numbness had set in. He reached for his snifter, downed what remained of his Cognac, and said, 'Why not?'